LONGING & CHAOS
CHAOS AT POLYTECH UNIVERSITY
BOOK TWO

CASSANDRA JOY
G.R. LOREWEAVER

Copyright © 2023 by Cassandra Joy & G.R. Loreweaver

All rights reserved.

No part of this book may be reproduced in any form or by any electronic or mechanical means, including information storage and retrieval systems, without written permission from the author, except for the use of brief quotations in a book review.

This work is intended as adult entertainment. It contains material of an adult, explicit, sexual nature. The author does not necessarily condone or endorse any of the activities described.

This is a work of fiction. Names, characters, businesses, places, events, locales, and incidents are either the products of the author's imagination or are used in a fictitious manner. Any resemblance to actual persons, living or dead, or actual events is purely coincidental.

Published by Saucy Pineapple Publishing 2023

Ebook ISBN: 978-1-957592-19-0

Print ISBN: 978-1-957592-20-6

10 9 8 7 6 5 4 3 2

A NOTE FROM THE AUTHORS

If you're a fan of Cassandra's Neighborhood series, be warned that though this series will end with a HEA, it is not wrapped up and tied with a neat bow in this book. Or the next couple. Be aware that you will have to get through a lot of chaos to get to the happy.

If you're a fan of G.R.'s Noctifer Witch series or have spent much time following #MondayMadness, this will not be a surprise to you. What you might find surprising is just how twisted this particular road is going to get. Hang in there. We promise it'll be worth it in the end.

There is BDSM. There's a sexual predator. There is blood play. There is… longing. Shocking, we know, since it's in the title. There are also lots of other fun surprises along the way!

There are also Easter eggs and jokes and puns and sarcasm galore, just like you'd expect from #JoyWeaver. There is passion and sex and awkward conversations and sex and heartache and sex. All the good things you crave from us.

We hope you enjoy this first series co-written by us. More to come. So much more in store.

For DW
Thank you for cheering us on, especially through the most chaotic days.
For our Beta Team
Thank you for putting up with our crazy chaos. You all are saints.

PROLOGUE

I ran a finger lovingly down the side of her cherry finish. My car was the perfect weapon.

Sexy. Strong. *Lethal.*

Just like me.

And she performed *so* beautifully.

I chuckled as I remembered the sight of Grayson's body, flying through the air like a sack of flour when I backed into him. The delicious crunch of every bone snapping simultaneously as he landed in front of my car. And how could I possibly pass up the opportunity to run him over?

Adding that glorious insult to injury.

I wished I could have taken his heart, but I knew it would be no good after smashing it with the weight of my car.

The whole scene had me deliriously horny. I nearly had an orgasm when the car thumped over his corpse.

Thankfully, I liked to be prepared and had a few toys in my glovebox. I was able to hold it together until I got about two miles from campus.

Then I couldn't take it anymore.

I pulled over and fucked myself hard on two of my favorite toys.

But that *still* wasn't enough.

I was a goddess of insatiable lust.

Thankfully for me, the bar close to campus proved to be a hot spot for males just begging to be fucked by a woman like me.

I found Owen at the bar and knew he was the perfect catch.

He was tall and broad. Handsome enough features and full of muscle. With a cock that tented his tight jeans quite well.

It took nothing at all to convince him that if he could show me a good time whenever the mood struck, that I would be inclined to elevate his grade to something that would look much better on his college transcript than the D+ he currently sported.

Smiling at myself and my cleverness, I waltzed back out to my murder machine and let Owen fuck me right there in the parking lot. In the dark, he couldn't even see the scratches on my baby.

Thankfully, the stupid boy paid no attention to the fact that Grayson's name slipped my lips when he finally managed to make me come.

Fucking Grayson.

The only thing that kept me smiling, was knowing that I was finally done with that asshole.

1
PRESCILLA BENNETT

*I*n the movies, especially the old black and whites that I adore, when a woman faints it's quite the theatrical affair.

She presses a hand to her forehead, sighs dramatically loudly, and collapses onto a random chaise that appears out of nowhere. If she's lucky, she may even faint into the arms of a handsome beau.

However, in real life… none of that shit happens.

Instead of a hand to the forehead and a sigh, you get wide eyes, panic, and sometimes a garbled response. You also don't fall gracefully back into handsome arms or cushy furniture. Most of the time, you fall onto a hard floor.

If you are super lucky, like me, you smack your head on the edge of the coffee table on the way down.

Ten out of ten, do not recommend.

Guys, if you can faint like the dainty ladies in old movies, definitely do it that way.

I groaned like a starved zombie and grabbed the side of my head. It felt like I got kicked by a horse. Right in the temple.

When I pulled my hand away and managed to pry one eye open, I was relieved to see no blood.

That's a step up, at least. I mean, I have had that happen in the past, but then there had been a patch of ice and an unwise shoe choice involved. Nothing like ending a date in the emergency room getting stitches in your forehead.

That's one way to find out the guy you're dating has a serious case of hemophobia.

"Prescilla, can you hear me?"

Damn that was a sexy voice right in my ear.

I opened my mouth to say yes, but all that came out of my dry mouth was an unintelligible garble.

"Let's get you sitting up. Cary, can you get her some water?"

Water? Yeah that would definitely help this dry mouth problem.

What the hell happened to me?

"Thanks Cary. Prescilla? You should take a drink. Small sips."

I managed to put my hands around the cool glass, but the big hands didn't let it go. I wanted to grumble about 'having this all on my own' but, to be honest, it kind of felt nice to be taken care of for once.

I'd dwell on the whole irritation with being overly comfortable in the arms of the guy that turned me down later.

After a few sips, I was finally able to push words out.

I blinked up at Cary and Jackson, who shared the same concerned look as they gaze back at me. I turned my head and there he was. Meemo. His face was so close to mine. I could sit up just a tiny bit and our lips…

My head started to spin and I instantly felt nauseous.

"Here, try this." Cary shoved a tiny hard piece of candy in my mouth.

Cinnamon. Yum.

My stomach began to calm down, but I didn't risk moving again.

"What happened?"

No one answered me for a moment. The silence carried an air of importance.

Or maybe I was just overthinking everything with this fucking headache.

"How much do you remember?" Meemo broke the silence with his quiet question.

I tried to think. "Um... I remember seeing you coming home. I came over because it seemed like someone was in trouble. I saw–something. I'm not sure, but then I remember it feeling like the floor just fell away and I was falling. Then the pain and just darkness."

I stroked my hand across my temple again and winced at the sensitive tissue there.

Meemo stood, lifting me into his arms as he rose.

"I'm going to take her home. Her mothers will know how best to handle this. We can talk about– everything…tomorrow."

A soft pair of lips pressed to my hand and Jack's voice drifted like a lullaby to my ear. "He's right, darlin'. We will hash it all out tomorrow."

"Give them our numbers." Cary said as he passed Meemo a small slip of paper. "Tell them to call us if they need anything."

Meemo moved to the door, and Cary opened it for us.

The cool night air fluttered across my skin. I should feel cold, but it actually felt…nice. If it weren't for the centipedes tap dancing on my forehead right now, being in this man's arms on a cool night like tonight would feel like heaven.

Mom opened the door on a sigh and the good feeling disappeared.

There went my chance of ever having a free moment in the bathroom alone for the next twenty four hours. They meant well, but if they weren't hovery enough when I was fine, you did not want to see them when I was sick. Or worse…injured.

No doubt they would be keeping me up all night long out of fear of a concussion.

Why couldn't I have just stayed unconscious a little longer?

2
JACKSON MILLER

*A*s soon as they were out the door, I whirled on *Grayson-Jonathan*. "What. The. Hell. Happened?" I was really proud of myself for not yelling it. But I might have been clenching my teeth too hard.

"I don't know." He shook his head and looked at me with so much helplessness in his eyes, I almost caved.

No. He did not get to just look at me like a sad puppy if he murdered my brother. True, my brother was a total ass, but that doesn't mean I wanted him dead.

Sort of.

"Start talking," I growled.

Cary's hand landed on my shoulder, and he gave me a gentle push toward the couch. "Sit down first, both of you."

Not-My-Brother wisely sat in Cary's recliner on the other side of the living room from the couch. Cary sat next to me and wrapped an arm around my shoulder. Then he turned and looked expectantly at *The Pod Person*.

"Why are you in Jonathan's body?" I thought my voice sounded calmer that time. Hopefully. "You didn't kill him, did you?"

"Of course not!" He seemed truly upset I'd asked.

"Then what happened?" I threw my hands up. "Because from here, it looks like you killed my brother and took over his body!"

"I told you, I was on my way to get dinner." He shook his head. "I don't know what your brother took tonight, but this body is not working the way it should be." He paused for a few seconds, obviously thinking things over.

"And?" Cary prompted gently. He was way more relaxed about this than I was.

"He was stumbling around half naked. I don't think he felt the cool air. Or anything, really. I'm not getting tons of sensory messages from his extremities right now."

"We should go check out his dorm room. Figure out what he was doing," Cary mused.

"I can tell you what he was doing," I shook my head. "Being a giant ass." I waved at Jonathan's crotch. Jonathan's shorts were not hiding a single thing. "He took something to get stuck like that. No hard-on should last through death *and* repossession."

"Are you sure about that?" Cary smirked. I groaned and glared at my boyfriend. How could he make jokes at a time like this?

"Please tell me you aren't feeding off of my brother's body right now," I pleaded. "You have better taste than that!"

"You're right," Cary threw back his head and laughed. "Jonathan tastes like an off-brand sour version of you. And I'm so not here for that." He turned to *The Imposter*. "Do you want me to see if I can siphon some of that off, though? Maybe relieve some of the pressure?"

"Would I prefer not to have a massive dick pointing at everyone in the room?" He shuddered. "Yes, please. Your brother is seriously packing, Jackson. Is this normal for vampires?"

I could feel a blush start to creep up my neck, but before I could say anything, Cary was laughing again.

"I'll teach you how to use it so that it'll be your biggest attraction," he promised *The Body-Snatcher*.

Gabrielle Anwar and I both groaned at the pun. "Just get rid of it for now," he begged.

"No problem," Cary said. But his lip was curled up in distaste. He really didn't like Jonathan's flavor.

Cary stepped forward and placed a hand on Jonathan's knee. I could feel the pull of his incubus magic, even though he was focusing on Jonathan's body. I watched in morbid fascination as Jonathan's dick slowly deflated. He sagged back into the couch as a sigh escaped him.

"Thanks, man," *Christine Elise* nodded.

"Well, that was interesting," Cary hummed as he stepped back from him.

"What?" I asked.

"I only got an aftertaste of Jonathan. Most of that tasted like Grayson."

"You've tasted me before?" *Freaky Friday* looked up at Cary with shock in his eyes.

"It's kind of hard not to when you're projecting sexual tension, man." Cary shrugged like it was no big deal.

"And when have I done that?" *Jamie Lee Curtis* certainly sounded like it was a big deal.

"Once you were on the phone right before we started class." Cary had a sly grin. "I don't know who you were talking to, but when you hung up with her, you'd filled the whole room."

Not-Lindsey-Lohan sighed and shook his head. "Okay, whatever. Thank you for taking care of…" he waved his hand at Jonathan's crotch, "that."

"Really," Cary patted him on the shoulder before returning to sit beside me. "It's no problem."

"Now, what are we going to tell my girl?"

"Are you sure she's yours?" Meemo asked from the doorway. The three of us turned to him.

"What the fuck, man?" *The Possessor* immediately yelled at him. Wow. I wasn't expecting that response from him. "Why wouldn't she be mine? I've loved her since we were kids!"

"She's my mate," Meemo said calmly. He still hadn't come all the way in the door. Which was probably smart because I felt like ripping his spine out through his chest right now.

Based on the look on *The Ghost's* face, he did too.

"Come on in," Cary said softly. "What do you mean she's your mate?"

"I mean my jaguar identified her," Meemo said softly. He closed the door and moved to sit on the coffee table next to *Patrick Swayze*, which I thought was a stupid move since now he was in striking distance of what was clearly a possessive male. But instead of showing fear, he looked at *Demi Moore* and asked, "How'd you end up in Jonathan's body? I'm really not understanding this."

"I got hit by a car," *Casper* sighed. Meemo's soft question seemed to leak all of the anger out of him. "Woke up in this body." He looked down at Jonathan's body wearing only shorts and flip flops. "You two are full vampires, right?" He looked up at me.

I swallowed heavily and nodded. "Yeah. From both sides."

"I'm a…" he paused and cocked his head to the side. "I was a dhampir. I think that's why I could settle into Jonathan's body. It was close by, but also close enough to my own genetics to work."

"This is so freaky," Cary groaned. "Major *Freaky Friday* shit. Your taste is kind of freaking me out the more I think about it."

I sat up straight. "Wait! If you're in Jonathan's body, is Jonathan in yours?"

The four of us looked at each other in horror. Who knows what kind of havoc my twin could create in Grayson's body.

"Grayson's body wasn't there. I only found Jonathan's body." Meemo shook his head. "He might have gotten up and walked away. I think it would depend on how he died."

"I got hit by a car," *Dr. Bruce Willis* said flatly.

I shuddered at the thought of Jonathan trying to accomplish anything in a fully functioning, but thoroughly maimed Grayson body. This was not a pretty image.

"We'll look for him in the morning," Cary said decisively. I turned and gaped at him. "No, Jack." He shook his head firmly.

"It's too dark and too late. We're going to bed now. We'll look in the morning after some rest. Once it's light again."

I rolled my eyes because all of us could see just fine in the dark, but the weight of everything that had happened in the last half hour weighed me down. Sleep sounded good.

"Grayson, go ahead and take my bed," Cary said. I stiffened next to him, but he reached over and patted my knee without looking. "I'll sleep with Jack until we figure out what to do with you."

"Can't I just go back to my dorm?"

"And have someone call the cops because Jonathan broke in?"

"Oh. Yeah." He hung his head as a shiver ran down his spine. "This is just so wrong."

"No kidding," I muttered under my breath. But before I could say anything else, Cary was pulling me toward my bedroom.

"Will you lock up, Meemo?" he asked over his shoulder.

I didn't really hear Meemo's reply because Cary had me through my bedroom door, closing it gently behind him.

"Talk to me," he said softly as he began to pull my shirt off over my head.

"My brother is dead," I looked into his eyes and felt an overwhelming grief I never expected to feel for my twin.

"We don't know that yet," he murmured.

"A stranger is walking around in my twin's body." I threw my hand toward the living room. "How can you say he's not dead?"

"Because we haven't looked for his body yet," Cary pushed me toward the bed and pulled the covers back for me.

"Am I an idiot for actually wishing my twin's alive?" I asked as I crawled into the middle of my bed.

"Of course not," Cary wrapped his arms around me once he was beside me. "You just said it. He's your twin. Your other half. Your evil half, granted."

I couldn't have stopped the laugh that ripped from my chest if I wanted to. "You're an ass," I said as I snuggled my face into his neck.

"But you love me anyway," Cary whispered.

"Yes," I laughed again. But then the laugh turned into a choking sob. And then another sob came. And another.

Cary held me patiently as all of the stress of not just today but the last few weeks of fighting with Jonathan all poured out of me.

He rubbed my back until I was down to just a few sniffles and I felt thoroughly wrung out.

Empty.

"Now, sleep." Cary whispered in my ear. "We'll figure all of this out in the morning."

But surely finding my brother wouldn't be as simple as that.

3
CARY CARPENTER

I wrapped my hands more tightly around my cup as a shiver ran through me.

We were far enough into fall that the early mornings and late evenings were cool. It was still frying pan hot in the afternoons, but the feel of a light fog caressing my skin chilled me.

I settled into a pool lounger and gazed at the woods behind the house while slowly sipping my coffee.

It had been a long night.

Jack kept tossing and turning, which meant I hadn't slept well. It seemed like Meemo had paced in his room for hours. I'd heard occasional groans coming from my room. When I heard him gagging, I got up to take Grayson a vomit bucket. It had to be hell to pay for the drugs that someone else took. But I thought he'd gotten most of them out. I hoped.

The sun hadn't risen above the trees yet, but soon Jack would want to be out searching for Jonathan. I had a gut feeling that it was a pointless task.

Where the fuck had Grayson's body disappeared to?

"May I join you?"

I looked up in surprise. Excitement warred with discomfort

to gain control of my stomach. Prescilla stood here in pajamas with a blanket wrapped around her. I just wanted to pull her into my arms and soothe away all the confusion and hurt on her face.

But how the hell had she snuck up on me without any of my senses warning me?

"Yes, please," I smiled at her. "How's your head feeling this morning?"

"Tender," she whispered. She'd brought her own coffee cup and sipped it once she was settled into the deck chair next to me. "Mainly confused. I feel like the world slipped into another dimension, but I got left behind. Or maybe the other way? I don't know."

I chuckled. "Welcome to the world of the paranormal. It's been right under your nose all this time." I thought about what Grayson had said and realized that was exactly how it had been. She'd been best friends with a dhampir since she was a kid.

"Are you serious right now?"

"Yes."

When I didn't say anything else, she huffed. "How the hell did Grayson get in Jonathan's body? Give me something here, Cary. Because I'm freaking the fuck out."

"What do you know about vampires?" I tried to ask it gently, but she still jumped back like I'd clipped jumper cables onto her.

"You're joking, right?" She asked. "They sparkle in the sunlight?"

I rolled my eyes. "No. I'm not talking about pop culture vampires. No sparkles or garlic aversions or anything. Be serious." I smiled really big to let her know I was teasing. "But real, live, living and breathing vampires."

"I thought they were dead. That they didn't need to breathe, and that their hearts only beat when they drink fresh blood. Although you are pretty pale." She wrinkled her brow.

"I am not a vamp! That's what I meant about pop culture," I laughed. "Jack isn't pale. Vampires are a species. Just like humans. Or shifters. Or…" I paused, unsure of her reaction. And I seriously didn't want her to respond unfavorably to what I was about to say. "Or incubi."

It was not a jumper cable to her skin this time. Her mouth just fell open slowly. "Incubi. As in plural of incubus. The sex demons?"

"Not demons," I sighed. "But, yes, we do feed off of sex and arousal."

"We?!" she practically shrieked. Then she started hyperventilating as she stared at the ground between us. Probably measuring how far away I was to see if she could run.

"Breathe," I said. I wanted to reach out and pull her into my arms, but I knew she wouldn't respond well. "Yes, I'm an incubus. Born to an incubus father and a succubus mother."

"Not a demon. Not a demon," she whispered. At least her breathing had calmed down some.

"No, not a demon," I grinned. "The only thing that makes me different from you is that I can…feed. Gain energy off of sexual activity around me. Sexual tension in the air." I paused to think about it. "And I've got a few extra bits. Like my horns."

"You've got horns!?" She was definitely shrieking this time.

I relaxed the glamor that kept humans from noticing my horns so that she could see them. She jumped back a bit.

"That's… okay." She shook her head. "You can put them away now."

I grinned at her.

"You really eat sexual tension in the air?" She looked thoroughly confused.

"And I can push some of that energy into whomever I'm having sex with. Whoever I want to make feel good."

"Whoever you want to control?" She narrowed her eyes. "Have you ever fed off of me?"

"No, I wouldn't *feed* off of you without permission!" I felt a blush creep up my face. "But… I have…sipped a few times. I promise that's just a reaction to sensing arousal, and not me, like, doing anything creepy. That's how I know what everyone's… flavor is."

She just raised an eyebrow at me.

"Some use it as a weapon, yes. But I was raised very differently. I hate people who force themselves on others. No matter what their species."

She nodded slowly. "So...vampires, incubi and...did you say shifters? Like werewolves? You're joking, right?"

"Are you going to ask that for every one of us?" I laughed.

"You're joking, right?" But this time, she smiled a little with it.

"Okay, okay," I raised my hands in surrender. "Yes, shifters. There are many kinds. But the one you should know about is the jaguar. They aren't as solitary as their wild cousins. They live in large prowls, often their entire village all related to each other and dependent on each other."

"So shifters. That would be Meemo then? But, he lives here alone. Unless he has family nearby?"

I was insanely proud that she'd figured that out. "Yes, he left his family farm to make a different life for himself. His prowl, his family especially, wasn't very happy about it. We're doing our best to give him a new family now. But there've been some rough days."

"So...Grayson?"

"Dhampir. Half vampire, half human." When she just blinked at me, I went on. "I believe his mom was the human, though I'm not completely sure."

"Do vampires practice voodoo?"

It was my turn to blink at her.

"What?"

"I always wondered if Daphne was a voodoo priestess." She smiled. "She had that energy, you know? Even if she was an art gallery owner."

"Heh." I shrugged. "You can ask him. Now that you know about our world, he can answer more questions."

"So body jumping? Is that common in your world?"

"No..." I looked down at my hands and realized I was squeezing my fingers together too tightly. "This has never happened before. We're hoping maybe you can help us figure this out."

"Me? Why me?" Her mouth fell open. "I'm nothing special."

I chuckled. "That is the furthest thing from the truth, precious Prescilla." I smiled. "Yes, we're pretty sure you're 100% human, but you are very, very special."

She blushed a bit. "I'm not really that special. I'm not sure how I can help."

"I think you'll be surprised," I said before downing the last bit of my now cold coffee. "I think you're the key."

4
PRESCILLA BENNETT

I blinked at Cary. "I can't be the key!" Horror flooded my system at the direction of my thoughts. "I can't be the reason my best friend is in someone else's body!"

"Woah there. I don't know that for sure yet," he shrugged. "I just have this feeling."

Feeling.

Well, *my* feelings were running all over the place.

So was my brain. I *felt* like my body was filled with bees stinging at my skin, trying to get out.

"So you said Meemo shifts into a jaguar? But it can't be like– a full size one? I mean people would have spotted that by now." It sounded ridiculous, but if I was going to embrace this whole supernatural aspect as truth, then I needed to understand the logistics.

"I don't mean this to be insulting, but humans are generally… well, what I mean is… Humans sometimes struggle to accept something that falls outside of their norm."

When I raised an eyebrow at him, Cary tried again.

"So supes usually have heightened abilities. We can see a broader spectrum of colors. See better at night. Lift a little more than a human relatively the same size. We can also move a little faster. That fast movement is when humans usually see a blur and then when they look back and see nothing they disregard it."

"Ok, so if I see a figure standing beside a shed but when I blink and it's not there, I would just brush it off as a trick with the lighting. Like that?"

"Exactly." Cary smiled at me, and I couldn't help but return it.

Incubus.

My mind rolled that thought around in my head.

No wonder he and Jack had such vocal sex. *I bet Cary is good in bed.* I licked my lips at that thought. *Really* good.

Cary cleared his throat, and I met his gaze.

"I'm not sure what you're thinking about, but maybe tone it down just a little. I'm getting mixed signals here." Cary's voice was deep, and his face moved closer to mine.

And then I heard it.

The deep pants-pissing growl of an angry, pissed off predator.

Cary whipped his head towards the wood line and threw up his arms as he scooted away from me.

I looked toward the woods and found a giant black jaguar? Panther? Some kind of big cat stalking toward us. I froze.

"I'm keeping my hands to myself there, big guy. No reason to get all alpha kitty on me."

Cary tried for a joke, but the glare the jaguar sent his way had him standing and backing away.

"I got the message, Meemo. I'll give you two some privacy." Cary ducked into the house, as the jaguar continued slowly prowling across the patio.

I should have been terrified.

A normal person would be scared and probably run away. Although, with a predator, it wasn't smart to turn your back on them.

But I didn't feel scared. And I had no urge to leave.

In fact, I felt like I was stuck in my seat. Awestruck by the slick feline approaching me.

Meemo stopped a few feet away and sat with his tail curled around his haunches.

"Can you understand me?"

The jaguar bowed its head once.

Great. As if last night wasn't crazy enough, now I was talking to a giant cat that could maim me in seconds.

Well... if I was going to go down the rabbit hole, I might as well jump in with both feet.

"Can I– pet you?"

He sat still for a minute, and I almost took back the question. I feared I misstepped and insulted him somehow. I mean he wasn't just an animal.

He moved towards me quickly and stopped directly in front of me.

I sucked in a gasp.

Meemo was a big guy, and his jaguar was no different. He looked much smaller when there was space between us. Now that he had me basically trapped in this chair, I would be lying if I didn't say that I was a tad bit nervous.

And then I looked into his eyes, and it was like falling into a trance. They're...*his* eyes. Meemo the man. His eyes were breathtaking on him as a human, but even more striking on him in this form.

Sensing my hesitation, Meemo moved his head under my hand. Much like a housecat would when it wanted attention.

"Oh, Meemo." I sighed and spread my fingers through his fur. "You're so soft."

I continued running my fingers through the silky, spotted coat. He must be enjoying the sensation too because he started purring. Loudly.

I found myself relaxing a little, but then more feelings began to tug at me. And the most predominant one right now? Hurt.

I pushed his head off my lap, and he looked up at me, shocked.

"You kept this from me." I whispered to him.

He hung his head in response.

"Meemo, I just found out that the world I have been living in is painted in faded hues, and that there is this whole other side that is vibrant and alluring. But you." I say in an accusing tone, pointing at him for emphasis. "You were going to just keep me in the dark. I thought you liked me?"

I pushed myself out of my chair and moved away from the jaguar.

I needed the room. I needed to pace.

Back and forth and back and forth. My anger built.

"It's bad enough that someone I thought had been my best friend was apparently keeping all of this from me our whole lives, but Meemo… Dammit! I was falling for you. Maybe I still am, I don't know. But you were just going to what? Date me? Knowing that I am completely oblivious to this side of you? Oh wait. That's right! You didn't want to date me! You were running from me."

I was angry at first, but now my movements were jerky. My many emotions were warring for control.

I was hurt. I felt stupid. I was a little scared. I was still a tiny bit worried that I'd hallucinated all of this and actually had a mental breakdown. I was a little turned on at the thought of real life paranormals. And I was angry. So angry.

I wasn't quite sure who all of those emotions were directed at most, and I think that just made it all worse. Grayson? Meemo? Myself?

Suddenly, a large pair of hands grasped my forearms and whirled me around. In a breath I was pressed up against Meemo.

A human Meemo. A very *naked* human Meemo.

His lips crashed against mine and stole all thought. My brain turned to mush and my nerves came alive— shot ripples of goosebumps across my entire body.

I didn't even fight it this time.

I gave in.

I hopped up, wrapping my legs around his torso as he caught me with two firm hands on my ass.

I kissed him back until I gasped for air but begged for another taste of him. Something inside me chanted for it.

More. More. More.
And then it happened again. Louder this time. Deafening.
One single word that stopped my heart from beating.
One word echoing through my very soul, that felt so right and yet so terrifying.
Just. One. Word.
Mine.

5
GUILLERMO PÉREZ

I felt it.

The moment she tensed.

Part of me couldn't help but wonder if she heard the thoughts running through my head.

The word that overwhelmed it all in the seconds before she tensed.

Mine.

I wish I could tell my jaguar *no.* I wish I could make him understand that things need to happen slower for her.

She just learned about this side of our world. She needed time to adjust. And… she was a human.

How the hell my true mate could be human was a curiosity all its own.

I pulled my head away from hers, but kept my grip firm on her plump little ass.

Her breathing was ragged, but she didn't look at me with fear and panic in her eyes like she did the other night when we kissed. This time, it was more of a question.

"I was an idiot to run from you. I'd already decided that yesterday before I found… Jonathan's body." I watched her carefully as my words sank in. "My animal calls to you. He wants to claim you as his mate."

She bit her lip and nodded. "Yeah, something keeps feeling so… right when I'm with you. Like something in my head screams the word 'mine.' Which is crazy since we barely know each other. Right?"

Hope bloomed in my chest.

She wasn't rejecting me. She just needed things to slow down.

I could give her that much.

"It is odd with a human involved, which doesn't happen that I am aware of." I kept watching her eyes. "But I am patient. I am willing to take things as slowly as you would like."

Waiting for that moment when she rejected my offer. Bracing my heart for the dismissal. She didn't ask to get pulled into the supernatural world, let alone be permanently bonded to a supe.

Instead, she blushed and nodded her head.

"We don't have to go *too* slow." Prescilla took a deep breath. "I'm not sure what the point of no return is, but I would like to know before then so I can make that choice. But we could spend time getting to know each other more." She ran her hand down my chest and I didn't suppress the shiver. "We could spend time exploring each other more."

"I'm a virgin!" That was a million miles away from anything I actually wanted to blurt out at this very moment.

Instead of– well, I didn't really know what I expected. Most guys my age weren't virgins. So I guess I expected pity? Horror? Shock?

Anyways, she just smiled at me sweetly. Almost endearing.

She leaned in very close to my ear. "So am I."

My cock, which I just now remembered was on full display, went ramrod straight, painfully hard, and I couldn't fight the growl that came from low in my chest.

She threw her head back and laughed. "The growl makes so much more sense now. Fucking hell, it's still sexy though."

At the last part she covered her mouth.

I loved that we shared this same unprompted ability to say what we were really thinking to each other.

I glanced around and didn't immediately see anyone. Still…

"Let's go somewhere a little more private. We can– do some exploring."

I spotted a blanket near the chair she'd been sitting in. "Grab that blanket?"

She smiled and snatched it up. I wasted no time in picking her up and carrying her out to the woods.

They had become like a second home for me since moving in with the guys. I loved the peace and calm I got out here. And the smells made my animal feel at home.

I wanted to share it with her.

She started nuzzling into my neck as I walked to the clearing and the sensation made my knees feel weak.

When she started running her lips across my jugular and nipped my chin I nearly dropped her.

Keeping my wits– barely– I set her down. She handed over the blanket, and I spread it out on the softer area of the small clearing. She toed off her slippers and crawled onto the blanket.

I fought myself to ignore how she prowled towards me, and I became suddenly overly interested in straightening the corner of the soft fabric. I didn't think she meant the movement to be nearly as sexy as it actually was.

She didn't pause. She knew what she wanted and rode that confidence on all fours right up to my cock. I barely registered her intent before she sucked the tip right into her mouth.

"Fuck!" I groaned and grabbed a fistful of those silky dreads.

She didn't stop at all. She took me in as far as she could, and then hollowed her cheeks heightening the sensation as she eased my dick back out. She came off the tip with an audible pop.

I released her hair, and she tipped her head up to look at me. "Sorry. It was just begging for my attention, and I was dying to know if you tasted like peanut butter… *everywhere*."

I chuckled. "And what's the verdict?"

"Mmm…" She licked her lips, and my eyes tracked the motion. "Yummy."

She tipped her head back down and closed her mouth around my throbbing dick again.

It truly took every ounce of control I had not to thrust into her face. Or throw her down and shove myself straight into her pussy. I might've been a virgin, but my jaguar had some very… interesting visuals.

Fuck! If I didn't calm down, I was going to come way too fast.

I steadied my breath and calmed the blood that roared through my veins. PB continued to work me over with her mouth. She brought a hand up and gripped the base so that she didn't have to take quite as much of me in at once. She gave a firm squeeze, and I groaned into the forest air.

I continued to try and hold myself in check, but when she brought her other hand up and caressed my balls, I started panting heavily. Then she trailed a finger backwards and pressed on the smooth skin just behind my testicles, and my knees shook as I exploded in her mouth.

I meant to give her a warning, but she had me at her will faster than I could have imagined.

She slowly licked me clean and smacked her lips. Looking up at me with the most mischievous grin.

"Like I said before. Yummy."

I growled deeply as I lowered myself in front of her and pressed my lips to hers.

We wrapped our arms around each other and our tongues began to dance again.

I was a little worried about tasting myself on her, but my passion was too high to care.

After a few seconds, I pulled back and gently pressed her shoulders. She took my direction and relaxed back, until she was lying flat with a look of nervousness on her face.

"You are breathtaking." I murmured my thoughts aloud, and she blushed.

I ran a finger down the front of her pajama shirt, and when I reached the hem, I lifted the material up slowly. Two small perky breasts with perfectly pebbled nipples peeked out at me, and I wasted no time lowering my head to pull one into my mouth, inciting a small moan from PB.

I removed my lips and turned my attention to the other. Sucking it into my mouth a little harder than the first.

She moaned loudly this time and arched her back.

She tasted magnificent. But this wasn't where I wanted my mouth.

I detached and heard a faint whine.

Fuck, that was sexy.

I trailed kisses down her abdomen, and when I reached the hem of her pajama bottoms, I slowly tugged them down her thighs. She lifted a little and I pulled the pants all the way off, tossing them aside.

Damn. She hadn't been wearing any underwear. I licked my lips in anticipation, though my hands were shaking slightly.

Her legs were on either side of my body but I couldn't help myself from pressing her thighs wider. Exposing her wet folds. I lifted her left ankle and began to press kisses to the skin there, resting her leg on my shoulder as I worked my affections along the inside of her leg and up her thigh. When I reached her delicious looking pussy, I inhaled deeply.

Fucking hell. She smelled like my favorite dessert.

I surged forward and impaled her with my tongue. She cried out my name. The most glorious thing I had ever heard. My cat purred deeply in approval.

Careful to keep the ridges on my tongue from scraping her, I continued to work her over. Thrusting my inhumanly long tongue deep inside her, I reached up and rubbed my fingers in circles around her clit.

It didn't take long before she was writhing under me. I gave her nub a gentle pinch, and she plummeted over the edge. Her cries rang out through the forest and my jaguar purred with satisfaction.

With one last lick up her slit, I met her gaze with a smile.

She looked back at me, panting. Her eyes screamed back with need. With *hunger*.

"Meemo, please."

I closed my eyes hard. Fighting back against her plea.

"We can't. Not yet. It would mean more than you are ready for."

When she looked up at me in confusion, I reached my hand out to help her sit up. She grasped it, and pulled herself up close to me. Curling her hands around my bicep.

I sighed and scrubbed my hands down my face.

"If we have sex, it's basically us confirming our mating. There is no taking it back." I gulped.

Fear screamed inside of me that this was it. This was the point when it would all become too heavy for her. When she would pull back.

Instead, she relaxed, resting her head on my shoulder.

"So, that would be it, right? Like make us a *permanent* thing?" Her voice was low, and her face turned away, so I had a hard time reading her emotions.

"Yes. It would be a for life thing. For me at least. My jaguar would never accept another mate."

She rubbed her cheek across my arm. "That sounds bigger than just boyfriend and girlfriend."

"It is." I nodded. "Much bigger. Would you…" I swallowed. "Would you like to be my girlfriend?"

"Umm, obviously?" She grinned up at me. "But I do think we were right to stop. For now at least? It's a lot to adjust to so quickly. I'm not saying no to… the mating bond. Just not yet." Her voice was still quiet but confident.

My heart leapt and I worked to calm myself. She hadn't rejected me. My jaguar growled.

Right, *us*. She hadn't rejected us.

I kissed the top of her head.

"Let's get back so that we can help the guys figure out what comes next."

She looked up at me and smiled brightly.

"Only on one condition." Mischief twinkled in her eyes.

"What's that?"

"Let me ride you." Her smile faltered for a second before she threw her head back and laughed. "That sounded so much dirtier than I meant!"

I joined her. "I knew what you meant." I winked at her and leaned in close. "You can ride me whenever you like."

Her mouth was still hanging open in shock and amusement when I stood and shifted.

"So fucking cool," she whispered as she slipped on her pajamas and slippers. She gave one last tug to straighten her shirt before grabbing the blanket and gently crawling onto my back.

My jaguar purred in approval of the feel of her body against him.

We carefully made our way back through the forest path and headed to the house.

I could keep myself at bay enough to refrain from marking her as mine, but there was no way I was going on any longer without calling her my girlfriend…

I'd just have to try hard not to blurt it everywhere in my excitement.

6
GRAYSON LEBLANC

I stared through the kitchen window and watched the jaguar walk out of the forest lining the back of the property.

With *her* on its back.

I'd waited too long. I missed my chance.

I knew that the second I looked out and saw her jump into his arms. Kissing him the way she kissed me.

Even though *that* only happened in my dreams.

I sipped on the water and continued to watch. He stopped on the patio by the gate and she climbed down, petting him lovingly once more before disappearing behind the gate.

The cat turned its head towards the window, and his eyes met mine.

I glared back. I knew it was petty, but I was already having a shitty morning when I woke up and discovered that last night was *not* a nightmare. Let alone the all night puke fest as this body purged all the stupid shit its previous owner pumped into it.

I turned my back to the window and the shifter. Sipped my water some more.

Guillermo opened the back door and stepped in. Smiling from ear to ear.

Smug bastard.

"How about some clothes there, little kitty?" There may have been a bite in my voice, but I didn't give a shit.

I knew it wasn't the shifter I was mad at.

It was myself.

It's my fault that she didn't launch herself into *my* arms this morning. I had every opportunity, and I'd wasted it. What a fucking coward.

Guillermo didn't say anything as he headed to his room. Hopefully for clothes. I already felt bad enough about myself. I didn't need to add penis envy to the list. The guy was huge… *everywhere*. It was hard not to notice. Especially when he ran around naked.

Although– I pulled out the waistband of the sweatpants I wore and inspected the equipment I now had to work with. Not too bad. I could probably give the shifter a run for his money with this thing.

I let the waistband snap back in place and let out a deep sigh.

Not that I really wanted to keep this white boy's body.

I liked *my* body. I liked my own dick, dammit!

Hopefully this was just some weird little backfire from one of Mom's protection charms or whatever. I never really understood her voodoo, but then again, she always said "it wasn't mine to understand." I guess that's because I was a dhampir, and she was a human.

Whatever the cause, I just hoped we could reverse it.

Cary walked in with Jack following behind. He looked–worn out.

I guess that made sense since my presence like this basically confirmed that his brother was dead.

And now I felt like a bigger dickhead.

Cary clapped his hands together. "Who's ready to go body hunting?"

"Sounds good. I'd really like to get back to normal. Although,

I guess I probably have some healing to do." I hadn't really considered that. I mean, I had been hit by a car, so I was sure there would be some damage.

Jack eyed me for a moment. "I can help with that."

"Thanks." I nodded at him.

Guillermo joined us in the kitchen just as there was a knock at the back door. Since I was the closest, I moved to answer it. Not even thinking about how this wasn't my house. Just operating on muscle memory. And it wasn't even my muscle memory. So weird.

She looked as wonderful as always. Except, she didn't greet me with the same warmth she had a few days ago.

"Hey, uh– Grayson. So are we ready to go find your body?"

Cary moved around me and pulled Prescilla inside. I wasn't sure why at first, but then I realized I had just stood there. Staring at her. I didn't even know for how long.

Geez. This weird time loss thing had better not be permanent either.

"Alright guys, let's get a move on." Cary called out from the front door as he and Jack stepped through. Followed by Prescilla. Guillermo just stood there. Waiting for me, I supposed.

What did everything feel so– muddy? Like I couldn't quite get a handle on what was happening.

To be honest, I was actually pretty scared of what we might learn when we found my body. The more I thought it over, the more I couldn't come up with any legitimate reasons as to why I would have body jumped to begin with.

Unless…

No, I wasn't going to go straight to the worst case scenario. That wouldn't help anything.

I finally got my feet moving, made my way out the door, and met the gang on the sidewalk.

Just as Guillermo shut the door to the house, one of Prescilla's moms came rushing out to us.

"Prescilla!" She folded her daughter in her arms and began sobbing. "Oh baby, I'm so sorry!"

Prescilla, clearly confused, started stroking her mom's back. "Mom, what's going on?"

She pulled back and took Prescilla's face in her hands. "We just got a call from the hospital. It's Grayson. He's–" She sobbed again, and Prescilla wrapped her arms around the distressed woman.

"He was so young. It feels like losing a nephew."

My heart shattered into a million tiny pieces at my feet, and I turned around quickly. Hiding the tears that threatened to fall from her heart wrenching words. I wanted so badly to hug her. To scream that I stood right here.

But I couldn't.

Guillermo gently placed a hand on my shoulder, and I jumped. I hadn't expected the gesture of comfort at all. Let alone from the man that I had just been snarling at earlier.

Clearly he was the bigger man, no pun intended.

"Guys, I have to go." I heard Prescilla soothing her mother as the two made their way back to the house.

"Well," Jack muttered. "I guess we won't have to search far. Thankfully, I have a few friends at the hospital."

It was on the tip of my tongue to ask him why he had friends there, when I realized it was probably due to his nutritional needs.

I was afraid to ask. Afraid that my own sorrow would bubble over.

So I simply stared at the concrete and nodded.

Cary and Jack took the lead, and Guillermo kept his hand on my shoulder, gently nudging me along.

Dealing with the death of a loved one was torture.

Dealing with your own death was worse.

What fresh hell did I body jump into?

7
PRESCILLA BENNETT

I sat on the couch, holding Mom and stroking her back.

At least the question of where Grayson's body was had been answered.

But I wasn't sure yet how I felt about his new body. Or the fact that my best friend had died… but hadn't?

It was all too confusing.

Momma Charlene kept fluttering around, bringing sun-steeped sweet tea and a plate of cookies. Then going back to the kitchen before pacing into the dining room. I didn't think she realized what she was doing.

"Do we need to go to the hospital, or anything?" I asked gently.

"No," Mom sobbed. "They said he's too torn up for us to identify. They called us because… because he had us as his emergency contact." A low wailing sound came from her, and I just pulled her closer to my chest, unsure of what else I could do.

I definitely couldn't tell them the truth. It was too unbelievable.

I slipped my phone out of my pocket and pulled up my contacts. I'd seen Jackson messing with my phone during our movie marathon the other day, and had later found his, Cary's, and Meemo's numbers all programmed in. I hadn't texted them yet since I didn't need to, but now was definitely the time.

Me: What the hell am I supposed to tell my moms?
Jack: See if they know anything about paranormals
Me: Like… that you all exist?
Cary: Exactly like that. Just see what you can get from them, gorgeous.

I sighed and put my phone down, then turned to Momma, still pacing between the dining room and kitchen. "Momma, did Daphne have any family? Anyone we need to contact?"

"No," Momma shook her head. "It was just Daphne and Grayson."

"What about his dad?"

"Oh, he left before Grayson was born, dear," Mom sat up and sniffed. "I don't think he was around very long. Daphne never talked about him."

Well, rats. That line of questioning was out then.

"I was thinking about her the other day," I said. How to ask, how to ask? "How I always felt like she was probably a voodoo priestess, or something. Her energy didn't feel entirely human…" I trailed off, leaving the thought hanging there.

Momma threw back her head on a laugh. "Well, you got that right!"

My mouth fell open and I gaped at her. "What?"

"She was very much into voodoo," Momma grinned. "And very good at it too. But, no. She was entirely human."

I blinked for a moment. Did Momma…? "You say that like there are people walking around here that aren't human."

"Oh, don't be silly," Mom tried to smile, but it looked watery. "Voodoo practitioners are human. What else would they be?"

I shrugged. "Shapeshifters? Vampires? Demons?" I didn't think Daphne was any of those, but I wanted to see their responses.

Mom did laugh this time. "None of those things are real, dear."

Momma kind of hummed in the back of her throat before

clearing it and saying, "But she was very good at making charms and– well… hexes. So I'm not surprised you picked up on that energy."

Before I could reply, my phone buzzed next to me.

Jack: What did they say? Do they know anything about us?

Me: They don't think paranormals are real.

Meemo: This is Grayson. Did you ask about my mom?

Me: Yeah. They said she was a voodoo priestess.

Meemo: I always wondered if they knew.

Me: What? She was? For real?

Cary: Anyway, you'll have to be very careful not to reveal anything to them yet. I'm so sorry we've got to ask you to hide this from them.

Me: I figured. Pitchforks and torches and all.

Jack: Dracula is one of the scariest movies I've ever seen.

Me: Uh, I was thinking more Salem Witch Trials, but…

When I chuckled, Mom looked over my shoulder. "Who are you texting?"

I jumped a little before clearing my throat. "The guys next door. Cary said he and Grayson had a class together. He's hung out with them before."

"Oh no!" Mom looked stricken. "And I just blurted that out in front of them!"

I patted her knee. "It'll be okay, Mom. I have a feeling they already knew."

Luckily, neither of my moms asked why I thought that. Because I knew I couldn't say, "Because Grayson was standing there wondering what had happened to his body!"

This sucked.

8
JACKSON MILLER

The four of us stood around Grayson's body and just... stared.

There was nothing to say. Nothing to do. Just a whole lot to process.

Because this didn't look like a mere hit and run.

No. This looked more like he'd been tied to the back of a car and driven down a gravel road. For over a hundred miles. At top speed.

Whether or not I liked it, I didn't think my brother was going to get his body back. Which meant we were stuck with *Jacob Marley*.

Maybe I should actually start calling him Grayson now?

I mean, it's pretty obvious this whole thing wasn't his fault. Or choice. I still didn't have to like it though.

I swallowed, forcing down the bile that had been trying to force itself up through my throat. "I don't think you're going to want that body back, bro," I finally managed to rasp out.

"I'm not your bro," Grayson said. Probably on reflex. But the assistant coroner who'd just come up behind us snorted. Grayson looked up at her and raised an eyebrow.

When Cary started laughing, Grayson turned his stare on him. "You're literally his twin," Cary gasped out.

Grayson blinked for a second then said, "Damn. I am not going to get used to this."

"Um," the assistant cleared her throat, "how do you all know the deceased?" She was probably confused since Cary just *might* have sent a few of his pheromones her way to convince her to let us in.

"We're his friends," Meemo spoke up quickly. "Since he doesn't have any family left, we're here for him."

Again, Grayson raised an eyebrow, but this time at Meemo. Apparently Grayson could control Jonathan's body just fine because I'm fairly certain my brother had never been able to raise just a single eyebrow. But Grayson was.

Meemo just shrugged at him.

"I hope he wanted to be cremated," the assistant said. "If not, definitely consider a closed casket."

"Yes. Cremation." Grayson gulped. "That sounds like the… only option."

Meemo reached up and patted Grayson's shoulder. Cary wrapped an arm around his waist, but I just glared at Cary instead of trying to soothe Grayson. My brother might not be coming back, but that didn't mean I had to trust his body's new rider.

"Were you two together?" the assistant asked softly. We all turned to look at her, but she was looking up at Grayson with soft eyes.

"What?" His brow furrowed.

"Oh, I'm sorry. I didn't mean to assume." She blushed. "You just look more distraught than the others. And they're all comforting you."

Immediately, Meemo and Cary both dropped their arms and stepped away from Grayson. I tried not to laugh. Or cry. I wasn't sure what this pressure building up inside me was. But I needed to get out of here.

"Excuse me," I said and stepped out into the hall. I tried taking deep breaths, but my racing heart would not slow down.

My brother was dead.

Well and truly dead. And his body had a back seat driver instead. A Ghost Rider.

Before the hysterical laughter in my head could make it out of my mouth, I pulled out my phone and opened the text chat with Prescilla in it.

Me: Would it be wrong for me to call him Frankenstein now? The people came after him with pitchforks and torches. Seems kinda appropriate at the moment.

Gorgeous: No, you cannot call Grayson Frankenstein. After all, it was his Monster, not the scientist that was chased.

Sex God: Not quite yet. We should let him grieve first.

Me: Grieve what? He's the one that's still here.

Kitty Cat: Maybe his body?

Kitty Cat: No, you may not call me Frankenstein. Or his Monster. Why the hell aren't I in this chat?

Sex God: Do you know where your phone is?

Kitty Cat: …

Sex God: I think the coroner is done flirting with you. We should probably leave now.

Kitty Cat: …

Gorgeous: Come home safe. I'll have the moms make something good for us all to eat.

I looked up from my phone as the three of them came out the door.

"May I have my phone back now?" Meemo asked Grayson as we started heading out of the building.

"Let me say one more thing to Prescilla…" he was texting furiously, but when he handed the phone back to Meemo, the group text didn't buzz. Seems like he had secrets to hide.

"What did you say to her?" Woah. Was that my voice? Why did I sound so… irate?

"Just asked for my favorite meal that Loretta cooks." He shrugged as he climbed into Cary's car.

"I want to know how you knew to jump into my brother's body," I demanded as I pulled the car door closed and reached for my seatbelt.

"Jackson," Cary said softly. "Leave him alone."

"No," I yelled back. "I want to know why the hell my brother is dead while this asshole is alive in someone else's body!"

9
CARY CARPENTER

I placed my hand on Jack's knee and turned toward Grayson and Meemo sitting in the back. "We're all trying to figure that out, love. And yelling isn't helping anything."

Jack turned toward the front windshield and stared out of it. Without my saying anything, he began a slow breathing count. Four seconds in. Hold. Four seconds out. Hold.

Good.

I turned on the car and put it in drive. Once I was out on the road, I quickly glanced at Grayson in the rearview mirror. "I've been thinking about this, and I have an idea."

Grayson jumped a little in his seat, then turned to look at me through the mirror. "What's your idea?"

"This morning, when we were having coffee together, Prescilla mentioned that she wondered if your mom was a voodoo priestess. Because of her energy."

Grayson's mouth fell open. I chuckled as I concentrated on the road again. I was fairly certain Grayson could figure out the rest of my line of logic from that. For an artist, he was seriously one of the most logical thinkers I'd ever known. The only one that could come close was…

Meemo grinned. "That would actually make a lot of sense if she was. She could have put a protective charm on you or something."

"She was," Grayson's voice was filled with awe. "How the hell did Prescilla know that?"

"You know, for a human, she's incredibly perceptive," I shrugged. "Once I laid out the possibility of paranormals being real in front of her, she figured out what most of us are pretty quickly." I smiled at her first assumption. "Once I told her I wasn't a vampire, that is."

Jack turned to stare at me, his mouth hanging open. "She thought you were a vampire?"

"Admit it. I look more like Lestat than you do."

Jack and Grayson snorted at the same time. Honestly, if you didn't know someone else was riding Jonathan's body, it was almost cute to see the twins acting in unison. They hadn't done that since they were toddlers.

It made me feel a little sad and happy all at once.

Yeah, his original brother was a slimy piece of shit, but maybe this would give him another chance at that kind of relationship. The one he deserved. Hell, after the loss Grayson had suffered, it would be good for him too.

A little chuckle came from Meemo before he swallowed it down. "Okay, so, voodoo priestess?"

"I wouldn't be surprised to learn she had put a charm on me," Grayson said. "But it obviously didn't work. Did you *see* my body? It certainly wasn't protected."

"No, but…" Meemo stared out the window for a moment. We all just waited. "Your soul was protected," he finally said.

Another simultaneous snort from Jack and Grayson. I wondered if they realized yet that they were doing that.

"Think about it." Meemo turned toward Grayson. "If you were a representative of the spirits, which is what voodoo is all about, wouldn't you want to protect your child's spirit, rather than their body? The body is almost… secondary."

"That doesn't make sense!" Jack cried. "None of this makes

sense! It's all crazy talk." He threw up his hands in the air and laid his head back on the headrest.

"Why is talking about voodoo any more crazy than any of us being paranormals?" I asked.

"Because *magic* isn't real!" Jack said it like that was the most obvious thing in the world.

"Uh, I think it's pretty magical that I can shift into my jaguar."

"Cary's incubus magic felt pretty real to me," Grayson added.

"Yeah, but those are traits inherent to their respective species," Jack argued. "But witchcraft and voodoo isn't an inherent species capability. It's not real. It's just parlor tricks."

I looked over at my boyfriend and began to wonder just how much Jonathan's soul being gone from this plane was messing with him.

Was Jonathan's soul trying to pull Jackson's with him?

The Aztecs had some pretty strange beliefs about twins, including that they were a single soul and couldn't be separated.

Whether or not that was true, the stress of losing his brother was definitely wearing on my boyfriend.

"Okay, we'll look at that option again later," I placated.

Honestly, I just wanted to get us all home. Then maybe back to bed because the coffee I'd had with Prescilla this morning was long gone. And I knew I wasn't the only one in the car that was wiped out.

"Oh my god!" Grayson suddenly yelled from the back seat. "What if I can't get back into my dorm room? How am I going to finish my art project that's due next week?"

"Uh, Grayson," Meemo said gently. "I don't think that'll be an issue anymore. The university is going to unenroll the dead student from all of his classes."

I glanced in the rear view mirror again to see Grayson staring blankly at Meemo. His voice had fallen to a mere whisper and the sorrow was thick enough to choke on. "How the hell am I going to finish my degree then? I was in my senior year... I only had five classes left to graduate."

"Well, now you're a junior in Accounting," Jack said dryly. "And you're likely failing."

"Oh my god," Grayson was whispering so softly that a human probably wouldn't have heard. "I wish I would have just died at this point."

"Enough of that," I said firmly.

I made a decision and quickly turned on the indicator to turn at the next light. "You aren't alone in this. We're going to help you. And the first thing we're going to do is move Grayson's *and* Jonathan's things into our house. It'll be easier for you to live somewhat normally if you have us with you, supporting you."

"We're going to help my brother's killer take over his life?" Jack's anger rose again.

"No. We're going to help the innocent victim of a hit and run build some semblance of a life from the ashes of two lives," I said with a bit of command growl in the tone. If I had to Dom Jack into helping Grayson, I would.

"I don't think I can do this," Grayson's voice was filled with despair.

"You can." I nodded. "You will. And that begins now."

I pulled up to Jonathan's dorm.

Jack stared through the window, grinding his teeth. I reached over and laid my hand on his. He turned it over to lace our fingers together.

Finally he nodded, but the snark in his voice was far from gone. "Okay, twin of mine. Let's move you back out of the dorms."

10
PRESCILLA BENNETT

Mourning was a horrible affair.
Whether it was a loved one that you'd been close to, or an estranged family friend, loss was never easy.

Do you know what's even harder?

Half-mourning someone.

Grayson was dead, and I sat here with my moms while they flitted around, making food and phone calls. Making final plans for a life snuffed out too soon.

And I just sat here. Confused and unsure.

I mean, it's not like Grayson wasn't still here. But then again, he wasn't?

I scrubbed my hands down my face, hoping to relax some of my features. My face felt sore and tense, and I hadn't even been crying.

Much.

Ok, I might have lost my cool a bit when Momma pulled out the photo album.

I must have still been holding my face, because Mom wrapped her arms around me.

I wanted to yell at her. I know, I know. It wasn't fair. But I just wanted some… space.

"Mom," I tried to get her attention, but my voice was muffled in her sweater. She must have heard me though because she pulled back and cupped my face.

"Mom, can I get some tea? I think I would like to go sit on the back porch for a little while."

"Absolutely, baby. You go ahead and I will get it all ready and we will come join you."

"No!" She jumped, and I winced.

I didn't mean to yell at her, dammit.

"I just mean– I think I would like some time alone." She smiled down at me and patted my head.

"Sure thing, baby." She seemed fine, but I knew I hurt her a little by pushing her away.

I really didn't think she ever meant to be so– *much*… it just kind of happened.

Sighing, I pushed off the couch and made my way to the kitchen.

Momma had moved into baking and prepping some things for dinner. I guess keeping busy was just how she coped with it all.

Mom handed me a to-go mug with tea, and when I raised an eyebrow at her choice, she shrugged.

"In case you don't want to sit still. That way you can take your tea with you."

"Thanks Mom." I didn't have to ask. She knew I paced while I dealt with things.

I stepped outside and closed the door behind me. But even with the space to breathe, I still felt far too tense. I just wished I could talk to them. I had always been able to talk to my moms about anything. And now…

Now I was keeping things from them.

I knew it was for their protection. I mean, I thought they would be okay, but I knew that humans as a whole wouldn't be able to handle this kind of information. That small safety you felt when you were alone, it kind of disappeared with knowing more.

It's not that I was scared really, but now I knew that the things going bump in the night might really be something supernatural.

So even sitting outside alone didn't feel the same. It didn't feel like I was really *alone* anymore.

I plopped down in the seat and took a sip of my tea. And another.

Nothing. I didn't feel any better at all.

I knew the guys were moving stuff out of Grayson's and Jonathan's rooms, but I really couldn't take the radio silence anymore.

I pulled my phone out of my pocket and smiled when I saw that there was already a message waiting on me.

Jack: This is so much fun. I'm so glad we are doing this instead of classes.

Me: I sense sarcasm.

Jack: Did it make you laugh?

Me: Maybe...

Cary: Why am I the one left hefting boxes while my big muscley man gets to stand around texting with a gorgeous girl?

Meemo: Grayson and I got the last of his stuff. On our way out, security told us that the campus is going into lockdown, and we have to go.

Jack: What? Why?

Me: Probably because they found a dead body? I had an email this morning that said all classes were canceled.

Cary: The school sends out emails?

Jack: I didn't get an email.

Meemo: I never even checked. I was... preoccupied this morning. ;)

Jack: If you aren't going to share details of your sexcapades then stop with the winky face.

Cary: Agreed. I think you owe us deets now.

Me: NO! No details of anything.

Me: Is Jonathan's room cleared out?

Jack: Yeah. All the incriminating stuff is out. We just tossed most of it in the dumpster.

Meemo: Trunk is full. We are on our way back.

Cary: I haven't even started the car yet.

Meemo: You know what I mean.

Me: Well when you guys get back here, we should probably sit down and brainstorm.

Jack: Yeah, we already decided that... Grayson... Is moving into Cary's "old" room.

Me: That's great but that's not what I meant.

Meemo: What's going on?

Cary: It's okay guys. I'm still sexy. We don't need to figure that out.

Jack: <rolls eyes>

Me: You guys... we need to figure out who MURDERED Grayson.

Cary: ...

Meemo: ...

Jack: Well fuck.

Cary: Heading home now. Meet us there. Let yourself in the back. Key under the flowerpot beside your back door.

I shook my head as I stood, then I stuffed my phone into the butt pocket of my jeans. I couldn't believe the guys didn't think about the murderer at all. I mean, there's no way that it was 'accidental' if Grayson's body was as bad as they said.

When I tilted the large flower pot beside the back door of my house, something shiny caught my eye. I bent down and scooped up the key.

Why in the world would they keep their emergency key over here?

Even if they weren't human, they were still totally weird. I bet it was Cary. That man's brain was always going in some unique directions.

I popped back inside the kitchen and found my moms right where I left them.

"Thanks for the tea, Mom. It hit the spot." I handed her the cup, and she offered me a sad smile.

I really wished there was more I could say to them. However, as open-minded as my moms could be, I still didn't think they could handle this whole world-tilting transition very well.

Shit. I didn't even know how I was handling it all so well. I was probably just going slowly insane, oblivious to the signs.

I couldn't even imagine how crazy Grayson felt. He essentially had a whole new body to get used to and a life to try and make sense of.

Oh! What about–

"Hey Momma, do you still have that bleach kit you changed your mind about?"

She exchanged a panicked look with Mom.

"Umm, baby. I don't think right now is a good time to make any drastic changes. I know you're upset, but–"

I waved my hand and stopped Momma's train of thought.

"It's not for me. It's for one of the guys. I'm going to go over and hang out with them for a while. Until dinner tonight, if that's okay. Then we can all hang out over here. Maybe help with anything else that still needs arranging?"

Momma smiled at me. "Of course, baby. The kit is under the sink in my bathroom." She patted her natural red hair. "I'm certainly not using it."

I chuckled as I headed to grab the kit.

Momma went through a very short-lived phase where she contemplated dying her gorgeous irish curls. Thankfully, Mom and I were able to talk her down.

I just hoped that Grayson would be up for a little make-over.

11
AMY GAMAL

I couldn't hide my inner glee when the dean announced classes were canceled today.

It was fun playing teacher, but no classes meant more *play* time for me.

I left the Fury at home and rode my Harley to campus today. The Fury had a few scratches in need of buffing. Not that I was worried about being caught or anything. I just didn't want the scratch marks to rust.

My baby had an appointment with her doctor for next week. It was the earliest Mac could get me in after I hit that 'deer.'

I shivered at the memory of all that blood. It smeared so prettily across the pavement when I backed up and dragged his body across the road a ways.

I found myself with a little pep in my step as I walked up the campus path. I had a student coming in for a *private* tutoring session, and since Owen was very well endowed, I had no interest in missing this opportunity.

The funny part was, I still gave Owen a B-, and he seemed happy as a clam about it.

Maybe I could get him to try a few new things if I threatened to lower his grade a bit.

My snicker was cut short when I turned the corner and smacked right into a huge wall of muscle.

"Oh geez. I'm sorry, Ms. Gamal." The guy chuckled. "We have to stop running into each other like this." He moved around me and snagged a box from another equally large guy before walking away.

I didn't know how long I stood there staring after him and his friends.

His voice was– *off*. Like a shoe that doesn't fit right.

I watched as his friends texted on their phones and he just stared.

At the exact spot I hit Grayson last night. Almost like he was transfixed.

I didn't know what pulled me, but I started walking in their direction.

They were still too far away when the guys hopped in the car, but I heard the smallest of the bunch call out to him.

"Come on, Grayson. Let's get going."

My feet stopped moving, and my body began to tremble.

No. No, it wasn't fucking possible.

I thought Grayson might have been a supe, but he always had this incredibly bland-tasting aura.

Unless…

Fuck!

He must be a halfer.

But how the absolute fuck did he end up body jumping?

"Fuck!" I screamed at the nothingness around me.

This guy was like a fucking cockroach, and he needed to be squashed.

I turned around and stomped my way towards the building again.

Owen better be ready for me, because I had a lot of rage to fuck out before I could come up with a new plan.

One where the asshole I murdered actually stayed dead.

12
GUILLERMO PÉREZ

When we got back to the house, PB met us at the door.

I pulled her in for a hug and couldn't resist snagging a quick kiss.

I didn't miss the tiny smile she hid. Or Grayson's hard scowl at my affections.

It was clear he had feelings for her. Why he never acted on them was beyond me, but I refused to back down. Even if I wanted to, my jaguar would never let me now that he'd tasted her. As far as he was concerned, she was already his.

"Well, if you guys want to unload, I will move all of my junk into Jack's— I mean *our* room." Cary wrapped his arms around Jack's waist and pulled him in for a sweet kiss.

I didn't mean to stare, but it was hard not to when they radiated love like that.

When I glanced at PB, she had a hand to her heart and a huge smile on her face. Yeah, she felt it too.

I didn't have to look past her to know that Grayson *still* scowled at me.

He was going to have to get over himself and either come

clean about how he felt to PB…or let it go. But if he told her how he really felt, I wondered what that would mean for us?

I would never stand in the way of her happiness, so if she wanted him–

But I could never let her go either.

This time I did look up and met Grayson's eyes. He was angry, but I didn't think it was all directed at me. I think he was angry at himself a lot, too.

So what if PB wanted him?

They had history. They'd been friends for a large chunk of their lives.

Typically in a prowl, mates were pairs. Granted that didn't always mean a male and female, but it was always two in traditional prowls.

But– I looked around at everyone here. I didn't live with a traditional prowl anymore. So maybe– I didn't know. Maybe PB could have however much love she really wanted. I wanted her to have all the love she needed.

My jaguar didn't seem upset by my line of thinking, but when everyone started to move, I decided to put those thoughts away for now.

Besides, I should focus on building the relationship I had with my girlfriend first.

Even just thinking of how she was my *girlfriend* now had me swaggering down the steps.

"You two look… nice together." Grayson's words came out with a bite, but it was meant as a compliment.

"Thanks, man." I knew it was a lame response, but what was I supposed to say?

A look of defeat washed over his face, and I resisted slapping myself. The dude had much more going on than just his woes for the girl.

For fuck's sake, Meemo, he was murdered! Say something supportive!

"Hey man, don't worry. We will figure this all out."

He ran his hand over his head, getting his fingers tangled in his silky hair and looked instantly disgusted.

"What is with this hair?"

"Well, it's yours now, so I am sure you can make some changes." I tried to sound encouraging, but taking on a new body *had* to be the weirdest shit ever.

"Yeah, well too fucking bad I can't undo some of these tattoo choices."

This time Jack laughed, and since he had been far less than his usual happy self today, it was a reassuring sound.

"My brother was a fucking idiot. I guarantee you he didn't have a good reason or meaning behind ninety percent of the ink he got." Jack shook his head and grabbed another box.

"So then maybe you can get them covered-up? Or altered or something?"

Grayson's gaze went distant for a moment before he nodded.

"Yeah, I can probably figure something out. I need to get this hair thing taken care of first."

PB chimed in at that.

"I was hoping you would say that! I brought some stuff with me. I can start in on that while we try to solve your murder." She clapped her hands together in excitement, clearly oblivious to what she had said and how that would sound to anyone else listening.

Grayson cracked a small smile at her. "Alright, Prescilla. Give me a makeover."

She chuckled, and we grabbed the last of the boxes.

Maybe a makeover would help Grayson start to adjust to this new body, because I honestly thought he was stuck with it.

13
GRAYSON LEBLANC

I had hoped.

I really truly had all of my fingers and toes crossed and had hoped against all hope. That I wouldn't be stuck in this fucking body.

But once I saw what was left of mine, it had become clear I couldn't get back into it.

At least if I had to jump into someone else's body, I was glad it was someone with a good support system. And let's be real: the height and mass upgrade was pretty fucking cool.

I knew it sounded crazy, but with every passing minute, I could almost feel my soul just– I didn't know how to describe it. Setting down roots? Like it was fully accepting this vessel.

We all wrinkled our noses when Prescilla came out of the bathroom with a bowl and paintbrush.

Why did I agree to do this again?

She beamed that beautiful smile right at me.

Oh yeah. That's why.

"Now that I got a bunch of the length off, I can lighten it up before I give it a final trim."

"Now when you say 'lighten up', just how light are we talking here? Please tell me I'm not going blond." It was hard enough having hands and a body in shades so much lighter than I was used to, but to think about tossing in some nearly white locks to go with it? I tried to keep a look of horror off my face, but I still struggled to actually *care* about this body.

I knew I needed to accept it.

And I would.

Just... not yet.

"No! I would never do that to you. I diluted the bleach a lot. And I am not leaving it on for very long. I just wanted to bring you down to a medium brown instead of pitch black."

"And what's wrong with black hair?" Guillermo asked in a fake pouty tone.

I didn't have a problem with the guy. Honestly. I just hated that he had beaten me to the punch. I had been so close. So fucking close to finally making my move.

"So while we are doing this, maybe we could go over some of the details you remember from last night. See if we can find anything?" Prescilla sounded so damn hopeful.

I sighed heavily. "That's just it. I don't remember much. A guy," I gestured at my new body, "was having some issues. Looked drunk or something. So I went over to him and then nothing. Dead."

"There has to be more to it than that. Where were you?" Cary sometimes had this way of making it seem like he was the most mature person in the room. It was such an odd contrast to his usually playful persona.

"I was walking across the parking lot and heading towards that ramen place."

"Oh! They have good food. Oops. Sorry. Please continue." Prescilla ran her gloved fingers through my hair, and I nearly moaned. That's so damn comforting.

"Yeah, so your brother was on the other side of the road. Crossing the quad I guess. But he collapsed and so I went across the road to see if he needed help and then I was flying through the air."

"There was no honking or anything?" Jack was joining in on the questioning. It seemed he was finally willing to accept that I didn't murder his brother.

"Nope. None. Just boom– flying– then splat... Then I think I remember getting run over again, but it's all kind of fuzzy at that point."

"So then it doesn't sound accidental. Do you know who might have it out for you?"

I rolled my eyes at Cary's dramatics.

"I'm not exactly a social guy. I don't really interact with many people, so I don't know who could have been that pissed at me."

Meemo leaned forward in his chair and caught my attention. "There has to be someone. Even something small. Just so we can start making a list and crossing people off of it."

I scratched my chin but gave him a small nod. The movement earned me a whack to the back of the head.

"Hey, no moving. I'm creating art." She didn't really have any heat behind the scolding, and I could hear the smile in her voice without turning around to confirm it.

"Yes ma'am. So I guess Keith might be a little upset with me. He's my physics lab partner, and I have kind of been letting him handle most of the work." I shrugged in embarrassment. "But I really don't think it's him because he seems to like the work and prefers doing it all alone anyways. I tried to help once and he developed an eye-twitch."

Jack chimed in at that point. "Yeah, I know Keith. He's a good guy, just hyper-focused. We can eliminate him as a suspect."

I shrugged my shoulders, which earned me another tiny slap to the head. "Then I've got nothing. The only other person I've spoken to other than you guys are my teachers, and I–"

Murderous eyes swam to the front of my memory.

No. There was no way it could be her.

She was a teacher and... and I shut her down when she came onto me. She seemed pretty pissed. In fact, I remembered being afraid of having to walk past her to leave the coffee shop.

"You have a look on your face. Who did you just think of?" Leave it to the shifter to notice the subtleties of my expressions.

"There is one person that I guess I kinda pissed off? She made a pass at me, and I turned her down. Twice actually. The last time she seemed so– angry. It kind of made me nervous. But she's just a teacher."

Prescilla leaned down to my ear, and I had to work hard to suppress the shudder from her closeness. "We have to rinse this in fifteen minutes."

I nodded at her as Cary posed the next question.

"That's a really big risk… dating a student. What teacher was it?"

"We didn't date. I might have had some attraction to her at first, but she was just so… overwhelming. You would think an art teacher would be more relaxed than she is."

"PB, are you ok?" Guillermo looked like he was two seconds away from jumping over me to get to her.

When I turned around, I saw the horror on her face and the fear in her eyes.

"Is your teacher Amy Gamal?" She asked in a hushed tone.

"Yeah. That's her. Why?"

"She's the one who has a hard time taking 'no' for an answer."

I remembered the conversation Prescilla and I had in front of the library– which felt like ages ago. She had said that she was stressed because someone kept flirting with her.

"You mean *she* was the one hitting on you?"

Prescilla just nodded her head.

Her confirmation made my blood run cold.

Maybe there was something more to the horny art teacher after all.

And I didn't think it was anything good.

14
PRESCILLA BENNETT

"Hold up," Jack's face darkened into a scowl. "You mean there's someone... a *teacher*, that's been hitting on you and won't stop no matter how many times you say no?"

I took a deep breath. "Apparently I'm not the only one she's been turned down by."

"How long has this been going on?" Jack looked at Grayson. "To both of you?"

"First day of class." I shrugged. "She's been no worse than some jerk guys in high school were."

"The weekend before school started." Grayson looked up at me. "What guys in high school?"

"That's not the point right now." I waved his ire away. "The point is that there's someone that was angry that you turned her down. Angry enough to run you over?"

"What guys in high school?" Meemo asked this time. He looked even angrier than Jack and Grayson combined.

I threw up my hands. "None of you are going to go hunt them down because they don't matter. What matters is Grayson's murderer!" Were they not listening?

"So, you think it might be this teacher?" Cary asked quietly.

He reached over and rubbed Jack's back. Almost immediately, the tension bled from Jack's shoulders, and he sank down into his chair.

"She's the only one that's been angry enough with me lately." Grayson nodded slowly.

"So that's our best bet." Cary nodded. "Figure out where she was. What she's been up to."

Grayson snorted. "What she's been up to is taking over the art department! I swear more professors have disappeared in the last month than I've ever seen before."

"What?!" Jack yelled again. "How can no one suspect anything when all the teachers just disappear?"

"Most of them had *reasons.*" Grayson shrugged. "Took a tenured position at a different school. Retired. It's only when you line up spring semester's faculty with this semester's faculty that you realize just how much has changed."

"That's messed up," Jack said, shaking his head.

"I couldn't get moved to a different section of my class," I added. "She teaches all of them."

Jack and Cary exchanged a look. "Okay," Cary nodded after a moment of silent mind meld. "I'll try to find out who she is. Grayson and Prescilla, I'd suggest that once we have classes back in session that you skip hers."

"I won't even have hers anymore…" Grayson sounded so dejected that I couldn't help but reach out and wrap my arms around his shoulders.

"Right," A light blush crept up Cary's face. "Sorry, man."

"I don't like that you've had to say no repeatedly," Meemo muttered.

His eyes were on my arms around Grayson, but he hadn't moved to stop the hug. He seemed more curious about the interaction than jealous. He smiled at me, like he accepted or approved of me embracing another man. Like he wouldn't mind if there were more men in my life.

I wondered what that was all about, and why the hell were my thoughts wandering in this direction?

I straightened, pulling away from Grayson.

"It's not like she forced herself on me," I sighed. "Just… made things awkward."

"Then why were you running like the devil was on your heels?" Grayson asked.

I opened my mouth to reply. But nothing came out.

I had no reason, except that she'd seriously creeped me out.

At least she hadn't tried to murder me?

Fuck!

"Is she going to come after me since I've turned her down twice?" Why was my voice so high-pitched?

All four guys sat up straighter and stared at me.

"I don't want you going anywhere without one of us," Meemo said firmly. "Whether this is her normal standard procedure or just something she did specially for Grayson. You shouldn't be where she can get to you."

I nearly rolled my eyes at his overprotectiveness… but a frisson of fear was running up and down my spine.

I wrapped my arms around me at the thought of Ms. Gamal trying to run me over. Or succeeding.

I was finally able to choke out a reply past the lump of fear in my throat. "Okay. I'll stay with you all."

It wouldn't be easy to juggle all of our class schedules. But I certainly didn't want to be alone with a murderer on the loose. A murderer that likely had it in for me just as much as Grayson.

15
CARY CARPENTER

*A*s Prescilla finished Grayson's makeover, I couldn't help but smile. "Man, you were sexy before. And Jonathan… wasn't. But I gotta say you in Jonathan's body is incredibly sexy."

Jack reached out and lightly backhanded my stomach. I left out a puff of air and laughed.

"I really didn't need to know that," Grayson deadpanned.

It made me smile even more.

"I…agree," Prescilla said as she looked Grayson up and down. "Not that you weren't sexy in your body," she rushed to add.

We all laughed at that. But that's when her phone rang.

Before I knew it, we were all around the table at Prescilla's house, having dinner with her moms. And trying to remember to call Grayson *Jonathon*.

After Grayson apologized for "his" behavior. There was a tense moment or two when Prescilla's mom saw him enter the house with us.

Poor Grayson. Paying for someone else's sins.

After his apology, though, we settled in and had a fairly good dinner. But the whole time, I watched the way Jack interacted with "Jonathan."

Some moments, it was like Jack was overcome with grief.

He couldn't barely look at Grayson without pain flashing through his eyes. Other times, it was like he was doing everything he could to hold in his anger and not yell at every little move Grayson made.

Poor Jackson. Getting his brother back, but not.

By the time we gave all the ladies hugs goodnight and went back to our house, Jack was wound tighter than a drum.

Tighter than a bow string.

Tighter than a high line wire.

As quickly as I could and still be polite, I bid goodnight to Grayson and Meemo and started pushing Jack back to our room.

My man needed some attention.

As soon as I had the door closed, I leaned up against it and just watched Jack. He plodded over to the bed and threw himself down on it, groaning while he did.

"Do you miss him?" I asked as gently as I possibly could.

Jack rolled over onto his back and looked over at me. "Who?"

I blinked a couple of times then asked, "Jonathan? Your twin who died last night?"

Now Jack blinked slowly. "What? No. I'm just tired from all of this activity today."

"All day you've been looking at Grayson like your heart got ripped out."

"No, I..." Jack scrubbed his hands over his face. "I feel guilty!"

"What?" I moved to sit next to him on the bed and ran my hand over his buzzed hair. "Why? Confess it all to me. Get it out of your mind."

"Because I *don't* miss him."

When I didn't say anything, Jack continued.

"I should miss my brother. My *twin*. The other half of my soul or whatever." Jack looked at me, begging me with his eyes, though I wasn't sure what for. "But instead, I'm *relieved* that he's dead. Relieved that I won't have to deal with his shit anymore. Relieved that he won't be leeching off of our grandparents. Relieved that I'm not going to get a call from the police in the middle of the night to tell me he's in the drunk tank or have to deal with any of his other immature messes."

I nodded for him to continue when he stopped.

"So now I feel guilty that I'm relieved instead of mourning him." Jack groaned again. "I know it's messed up. But I can't help it."

I let out a deep sigh and looked my boyfriend over.

I knew what he needed. The question was whether or not he'd be open to it tonight.

Finally I decided to just ask him. "Wanna scene?"

Jack's head whipped around so that he was staring into my face. "Right now?"

"Of course," I smiled.

"Please…" It came out as a begging plea.

16

JACKSON MILLER

Almost immediately Cary relaxed the glamour that hid his incubus horns and tail. A shiver ran through my body. My fangs descended, and my dick sprang to a semi very fast.

I needed my man.

My Dom.

The priest for this confessor.

I gripped my blanket, waiting for instructions. But more than anything, I wanted to fall to my knees before him.

And *beg*.

Beg for forgiveness.

Beg for atonement.

Beg for mercy.

Beg for a fucking orgasm!

I almost snorted at the thought. But if Cary was going to be my priest tonight that I confessed all of my sins to, then I hoped he was the kind that loved to give good boys a reward for confessing.

"What is that thought in your head?"

I blinked back to the present. "Um... You really don't want to know."

Cary studied my face for a moment and then a wicked grin spread across his. "On your knees now," he said with a gesture to the floor.

Yes!

There were times I swore he could read my mind.

I scrambled to the ground and put myself between Cary's knees as he slowly spread them apart.

"Forgive me, Father, for I have sinned," I muttered under my breath. But I didn't touch him yet. He hadn't given permission.

I needed permission so badly.

More than my next breath.

A low chuckle came from above me. And with it, a blast of Cary's incubus magic washed over my skin and sank into my bones.

Semi now a full fucking hard-on.

I groaned, but held still.

"You were such a sweet boy," Cary ran both of his hands over my head so that he could grip the back of my neck with both hands. "Confessing your sins to me." He bracketed my jaw between his thumbs and first fingers. "Praying and pleading so prettily." He tilted my chin up so that he could look into my eyes. "I think you deserve a blessing for your penance."

Another groan ripped from my core. "Cary, please."

"Unzip me," he whispered. It was low and gravelly. Filled with his magic. The lust swirled around us, fueling this moment with a delicious tension.

I reached up to unbutton Cary's jeans and slowly pulled the zipper down. His cock immediately sprang free.

Damn. If I'd known he was going commando today, I would have jumped his bones much earlier.

"Fangs out." This time it wasn't a whisper. No other word could describe the command than "growl."

I grinned up at him so that he could see they were already dripping, begging to come play.

Cary shifted a bit as he shoved his jeans down a bit, giving me a better view of his quickly filling dick. Of his creamy thighs.

I swallowed another moan.

Cary's Jacob's ladder caught the light and twinkled at me. I licked my lips, wanting to taste him. Wanting to use that beautiful set of surgical steel to drive my man insane.

"Bite. Me." Cary grit out.

My heart soared, and my claws came out to play along with my fangs.

I reached up and grabbed Cary's thighs, digging the tips of my claws in. Then I leaned forward and sucked him into my mouth. Made sure my fangs scraped all the way down.

His precome exploded over my tongue, and my claws sank in deeper at the taste. Once I'd slicked him up, I slowly pulled off his dick, again dragging my fangs along the large veins running through his cock, running my tongue between the ball ends of his ladder.

When I reached the head, I gently nicked his slit before pulling off. I nuzzled back down his cock and beside his balls.

Then without warning, I sank my fangs into his femoral artery. When I took a deep pull, Cary moaned above me and gripped my head harder.

That's when I noticed that his claws had sunk into my skin as well. A trickle of blood ran down my throat and pooled in the hollow of my clavicle.

Suddenly, I couldn't get enough of him. I drank from him, inhaling his scent, his magic, his essence.

After a minute or an hour or an eternity, I pulled back to lick up his dick.

I rubbed him down, covering his cock and balls and thighs with his blood. I rubbed across his taint as I sucked gently on the head of his cock.

He bowed back, gripping my head tightly to him. His cry of pleasure was like the best benediction I'd ever received.

I kept my claws from his asshole because I knew he hated my claws inside him there. But I did grab big handfuls of his cheeks and sink my claws into them.

When I reached up beneath his shirt to tweak one of his

nipple bars while I also sank a fang into his cock, Cary moaned low and came.

I sucked him down, swallowing quickly so that I didn't miss a single drop.

When I sat back, I couldn't help the smug smile. Cary was so blissed out, struggling to pull in air, but with satisfaction written all over his face.

"Good boy," he said with a sigh.

I burst out laughing, resting my forehead on his quickly healing thigh. We had never role-played as a priest and confessor before. And we didn't do age play. But if "confessing" had him saying that to me in such a pleased tone, then I would be more than happy to do it again.

"My turn," he growled as his claws sank into my neck again and his tail wrapped around my waist. "Get up here, sweet boy."

I scrambled to obey.

17
PRESCILLA BENNETT

Sitting on the patio, sipping coffee with my boyfriend after an amazing meal– more like a buffet– that my moms made for us all, was such a wonderful feeling.

Boyfriend.

It felt so strange thinking of him like that. New. Exciting. Scary.

My eyes drifted from my cup to his chair.

He had pulled it close, but he hadn't tried to touch me yet. Part of me felt grateful that he wasn't overbearing and smothering in his affection. I loved the fact that he seemed happy and content to just sit quietly with me, sipping coffee, and staring off into the night.

The other part of me was a raging whore and wanted him all over me.

On me.

In me.

My skin broke out in goosebumps, and I tried to force my mind to think of something else.

I heard Meemo inhale deeply before his eyes flicked towards me, holding me still under his molten gaze.

Right.

Enhanced senses.

Enhanced smelling.

That meant I wouldn't ever be able to hide when I was horny.

Well, this just got a lot more interesting.

We moved in tandem, neither of us speaking.

Meemo slowly set down his coffee cup, and I followed suit.

We turned to face each other. He spread my thighs and placed his knees between them. As he continued rubbing his hands up my thighs, my breath began to quicken.

I was nearly overwhelmed with excitement and anticipation.

When his hands reached my ass, he took a firm hold before pulling me towards him. Our movements were so fluid. Like a sensual dance. Once I reached the edge of my chair, he continued to pull me closer until I straddled his lap.

He inhaled again, and *why* was that so fucking sexy?

I never thought that a man sniffing me would turn me on, but here we were. Learning new things every day.

As I settled my weight onto his thighs, his bulge tapped against my core, we both sucked in a breath.

Meemo started breathing heavily and leaned in, resting his forehead against mine.

"I want you. More than I have ever wanted anything in my entire life. Tell me the truth. Tell me you don't want me just as badly. Tell me, and I will hold myself back." His voice was shaking with his barely controlled desire.

And suddenly my mouth felt dry.

What did I want?

What did I really want?

"I…" I had no words.

Everything just felt so *right*. I wanted him. I wanted to make him mine, and I wanted to be his. I felt territorial in a way I never had before.

"I want you. From now until the end of eternity. For today and the next and every day that follows. It's not a decision, but rather what just feels like... fact." My voice trembled slightly at my admission.

We hadn't known each other long. Certainly not long enough for the *normal* versions of forever. But who the fuck cared about normal?

I was just a girl who was in love with a shifter. My best friend was a ghost– or zombie, we weren't clear there yet. And my other two friends were an incubus and a vampire. This was my new normal.

As freaked out as I *should* be, I just wasn't.

It felt like my life before this had been a sock that was always just a tiny bit too small or a teensy bit large. And now?

Now it all fit perfectly.

We heard a loud moan from inside the house, which I quickly recognized as Cary's, before a wave of heat rushed over me. My nipples became impossibly hard. The slight movement from the fabric of my bra made me gasp. Meemo shuddered heavily underneath me.

Like a lightbulb going off inside my head, the feelings all made sense. "That's Cary's incubus... *stuff*. Isn't it?"

Meemo pulled back and smirked at me. "Yes and no. He can intensify someone's attractions and their..."

"Horniness level?" I supplied helpfully, and he chuckled a bit.

"Yeah. That. Anyways, he can magnify those feelings, but they have to already be there. And moments like right now? He actually can't help that it kind of spills out." He shook his head and smiled. "When an incubus is... *happy*, we're all happy."

I smiled back at him. Really, he already got my engine going well on his own, but I didn't mind Cary's boost.

Something shifted in Meemo's expression, though. Clearly his thoughts had him worried.

He gripped my ass again and stood with me in his arms. He didn't miss when I snagged my blanket on our way up and smirked.

As he moved us into the woods, we stayed silent. The overwhelming urge to rip his clothes apart was gone. But my yearning for him was not.

Hopefully this change of location was simply to set the scene, because I was ready.

I was more than ready.

Give me what's *mine*.

18
GUILLERMO PÉREZ

I knew I confused PB when I moved us out to the woods, but I was trying my damnedest to be level headed here.

I knew she wanted me. I *knew* we were right together. But… I needed to know for sure that her feelings were not all just influenced by her enhanced lust right now.

Not that I minded her magnified cravings.

I couldn't fight him; my jaguar pushed me to inhale her scent again.

I had never been harder.

I stopped in the clearing we were in this morning. It was hard to believe it was just this morning.

Part of me feared that this all moved so fast, but the other part of me trusted PB to know what's in her heart.

Continuing to hold her, I forced the words out. Needed to hear her answer.

"Tell me this is what you want. Tell me that *I* am what you want." My heart was going to beat its way through my ribs and out of my chest.

She nuzzled her head against my cheek. "*You* are what I want, Meemo."

"I need to know that if we cross this line, you know it's forever. I mate for life." I swallowed hard.

"Meemo?" She looked up at me so fucking sweetly.

"Yes, *compañera*?" My voice didn't squeak, did it? Surely not.

Her eyes sparkled for a minute before they turned mischievous. "If you don't fuck me soon, I'm going to have to force myself on you."

I threw my head back and laughed. I set her down and took the blanket to spread it out.

She moved to me, and we began this slow torturous ritual of carefully undressing one another.

Stopping to kiss or caress.

The touch, feel, and smell of her were almost too much. She engulfed me.

We sank to our knees on the blanket at the same time, and then it was like something snapped.

We lunged at each other.

Frenzied lips and hands. We rolled around on the blanket. Both of us wanted control and neither of us were willing to relinquish it.

When my jaguar began to roar in my head, I sank my fingers into her wetness. Needing to prep her. To stretch her. To make her ready for me.

She cried out my name as I circled the pad of my thumb across her clit.

She moaned and writhed and became impossibly wet. God, she was going to kill me. My jaguar was pushing at me. He wanted his mate. Right the fuck now.

"Please, Meemo. Take me." She begged.

Four words.

That's all it took for me to lose any semblance of control over myself. For my jaguar to take over.

I pulled my body up to hers, bringing my cock to her entrance.

With one shaking hand I grabbed hold of myself and ran my tip through her folds.

Sweat began forming on my forehead, and I watched in awe as a tiny bead of precome slid from the head of my cock and joined in her wetness.

She moaned deeply, and I began to press inside of her.

I took things slowly. Both for myself and for her. But it took every ounce of control that I had.

I worked my cock in, pulling back a little ways, and then easing in some more. Please let this be good for her.

She reached down and gripped my shoulders. Before I even got a chance to warn her, she thrust her hips up to meet mine in one hard blow that had us both screaming out in bliss.

"Fucking hell *compañera!*" I froze. "Are you okay?"

Don't blow. Don't blow, Meemo. I held as still as I could until I wrestled down the need to come right fucking now.

She felt so damn good. My mate felt even better than I had dreamed. She was amazing.

"I would be better if you were fucking me. This is torture Meemo." She whined a little, and I couldn't help the smirk. Guess I hadn't hurt her as much as I feared.

I wasn't sure exactly where this cocky confidence had come from. Probably from my jaguar because Meemo the man was nervous as hell. And trying not to be a one-pump-chump.

I leaned forward and brushed my lips across the skin of her neck. I groaned as the shift in position brought me right back to the edge. She shuddered in response to the kiss. Or the movement.

"So is this torture?"

"Yes." Her voice sounded heady with desire.

I kissed down the valley between her breasts as I tried to ever so slowly pull my hips away from hers. Hands rubbing her skin to hide their shaking. Mouth traveling down to circle her nipple with my tongue.

"And this? Is this torture?" It certainly was for me.

Her answer was barely a murmur.

Once I was out as far as I wanted, I brought my mouth to her other nipple and sucked it in hard as I thrust my cock deep inside her. Another shudder.

God, her pussy was perfect.

She cried out something unintelligible and scratched her hands down my back.

That one primal act nearly had me coming undone. But I *needed* my mate to come first.. I had a firm idea how this would happen once I hit my release. And marking meant we would need to be in a different position.

So I clenched my jaw and held on. Determined to give her pleasure first.

I set a gentle but steady rhythm as my dick slid back and forth through her channel. I kept my attention on her breast and moved my spare hand down between us to rub my fingers across her clit.

It was pure torture. My jaguar hated this pace. He wanted to eat her up.

When I felt her walls begin to tighten around me, I picked up my pace a little. She scratched her nails down my back again, and I gave the nub a little pinch as I gently bit down on her nipple.

She screamed my name, and her whole body quaked. A tiny liquid fountain erupted from her pussy, and my mouth watered in anticipation.

As much as I enjoyed this, needed it for her sake, I *needed* to claim her.

I pulled back, my cock slowly pulling out of her.

She whimpered again, so I leaned up to her ear and kissed her lobe.

"I'm not done with you yet, *compañera*. I need you to get on your hands and knees. Show me that gorgeous ass of yours."

She hesitated a little, so I reassured her of my intention.

"I'm just changing our angle. We won't be doing any experimenting with other… areas just yet."

She leaned forward and bit onto my pec.

Hard.

Before giggling, turning, and shoving that fucking sexy ass right in my face.

I nearly came right then. Fuck it was so hard to stay in control.

But I needed this more.
I needed to *claim her*.

19
PRESCILLA BENNETT

I knew I was being playful when I bit him.

But I figured: *he shifts into a cat; he can take a little playfulness.*

I expected him to retaliate.

I did not expect my sweet Meemo to have a bit of a kinky Dom side.

He leaned forward and blew gently across my skin. Making it pebble with goosebumps. He continued this as he moved closer and closer to my exposed pussy. When he sent a wave of his breath across my asshole and straight down, I couldn't fight the squirming.

It was so fucking weird how good that felt.

When his mouth came back up, he latched it right to my asscheek. Biting me like I'd bit him.

I moaned and pressed back into him a little. He pulled his mouth away and slapped his hand down hard where his mouth had just been.

"Fuck!" I screamed out.

I couldn't believe how much I loved all this naughtiness.

He used both hands to massage my cheeks and groaned.

"You have no idea how fucking sexy this pussy is." He moved one hand down and slicked his fingers right through me.

I heard him suck the fingers into his mouth and pull them out with a pop.

"And fucking delicious."

Oh. My. God.

Was it possible to orgasm from dirty words and spankings? Because I was almost there.

Meemo gripped my hips, and I felt the head of his glorious cock nudge at my entrance again.

I pressed back into him as Meemo surged forward. When he filled me as much as he could, I sucked in the air between my teeth a little.

Why did his dick feel bigger?

Did it go in deeper at different angles?

I guessed that would make sense.

The near painful ache quickly ebbed, and Memmo began to move slowly.

I couldn't take any more of this glacial speed.

I felt like *I* was the cat shifter. I wanted roughness and biting and scratching and slamming his cock into me so hard.

I wanted to worry about ripping in two.

I planned my movements carefully, and when I felt him begin to surge towards me again, I slammed my ass against him.

Hard.

I didn't give him a chance to react, and I rocked forward before slamming back onto him again.

I never thought I would so thoroughly enjoy being impaled.

Suddenly I felt incredibly grateful for my one-night stand with the massive jelly dilly. It'd been good prep work.

Tomorrow's ache would be worth this moment.

Meemo snapped. He growled and slammed into me with reckless abandon. Fucking me mercilessly in a way that my soul craved.

Ah, there was his jaguar!

No... *my* jaguar.

When he angled his hips just slightly, I burst apart.

My body pulled tight as a bow string, and my walls contracted and squeezed his dick. The urge to come vibrated through me.

He paused in his glorious destruction of my vagina and let me catch my breath. But the second I had it, he started pounding me hard again.

His movements became jerky, and I knew that he was getting close.

Playing on instinct, I reached my hand under us and cupped his balls.

He cried out my name and clenched his arms around my waist. Holding me firmly in place.

It was almost like when he came his dick punched right into my g-spot.

So. Fucking. Good.

I didn't cry out this time, but my vision went blurry, and my body quaked against his even more.

A tsunami erupted between us as another release shot from me. In that second, Meemo surged forward and latched his teeth onto my shoulder blade, biting down.

It was too much. All too much. I couldn't stop coming. I felt like a star about to burst into a million tiny pieces.

And it would be a glorious way to go out.

Meemo's body relaxed a bit, and that's when I felt it....

Whatever was hitting my favorite spot finally relinquished, and something hard released its grip on my walls. Nothing uncomfortable, but definitely not expected.

What the hell?

He withdrew from me, and tugged me towards him as he collapsed onto his back. Curling me against the side of his body and making a sound that was suspiciously close to a purr.

"Meemo?"

"Yes, *compañera*?"

"What was that?" I didn't mean to blurt it out, but I felt so damn curious. "Was that... knotting?" I thought romance authors made that shit up, but that was the closest thing I could think of.

"Technically, they're called spurs. But I don't like the idea of wearing spikes to ride you." He yawned, and I decided to make a plan to investigate the hell out of his dick later. "It's hard to explain, but even in my human form, I'm not *all* human."

Unable to fight the call, my own yawn overcame me.

Why *did* that happen?

Why the fuck were yawns so…

Contagious?

20
GRAYSON LEBLANC

I should have been in bed hours ago.
What was I doing instead?
Watching.
Waiting.

It was none of my business if they slept out in the woods all night. But I couldn't help the jealousy that flooded me.

And what's worse? I wasn't even jealous that he was with her. Just jealous that I wasn't with them.

I'd been feeling this strange pull of camaraderie towards Guillermo– er… Meemo I guess, since I'd met the guy.

So no, I didn't care that they were together. I could feel that he was right where he was supposed to be. With her. I just wanted to be there too.

Another loud moan rang throughout the house.

Why did I think living with an incubus would be a good idea?

What's worse was that I felt too embarrassed to talk to anyone about my… issue.

While this body had no issues reacting to the lust blasting around this place, I couldn't actually *feel* that I had a boner. I didn't *feel* aroused. I saw it. And when I decided to stroke it a little, I definitely felt it. But it just felt… dull.

I wouldn't know that I had an erection if I hadn't looked down.

Well, that was good to know at least.

Maybe it was best that I wasn't out there with them. There was no way I would be able to perform.

And I didn't exactly know how I felt about finally actually fucking the girl of my dreams… with someone else's body.

Even if it was mine now.

I hoped this feeling passed at some point. I didn't want to go through life with this never-ending feeling that I was stuck in the wrong body.

I sighed and turned around, walking back to the room that was now mine. I walked in and closed the door behind me. I hadn't unpacked much, but I pulled my earbuds out of my bag and slipped them in.

Not that I was annoyed by the sounds of Cary and Jack. I just needed some time to escape my own thoughts for a little bit.

I hit play on my heavy rock playlist and let myself become overwhelmed with the music.

21

JACKSON MILLER

*J*had not wanted to get out of bed this morning.

I woke up wrapped around Cary's hot body with our legs all tangled together. I could have stayed right there for hours.

For *days* if Prescilla had been with us.

Someday, maybe.

Eventually I had to pull myself away from my spot nuzzled in Cary's neck so that I could get to class. It was still too early in the semester to start skipping classes yet.

Oh. Classes.

Poor Grayson. Suddenly stuck in boring accounting when he was an art student.

Damn.

Maybe we could get Jonathan's credits transferred? Who knew? That really was a problem for Grayson. I just had to get to Business Comm now.

I ran through the routine of getting dressed, brushing my hair and teeth, and grabbing an apple on my way out the door. I just might have skipped down the street a little more than normal, a leftover side effect of all the delicious sex last night.

Within minutes, I pushed through the doors of the language arts building, mind on how Grayson could solve his degree problem. And that's when I managed to run someone over. Great job, dick.

"Oh, I am so sorry!" I said as I reached out and kept the woman from falling to the ground.

I looked down into the dark haired beauty's face and felt my heart ice over.

"Um. I feel like you're madder than me running into you warrants," I cocked my head to the side, trying to figure out why her eyes were shooting daggers at me.

Then she blinked. And blinked again. Then her eyes landed on my hair. "Oh," she said. "Sorry about that. I thought you were someone else for a moment."

"Let me guess," I sighed. It wasn't like this was the first time something like this had happened. "Jonathan fucked you and left you and was a total douche about it?"

I didn't expect the delighted laugh that burst from her. "Actually, I walked out on him. The prick was more interested in watching himself in the mirror than making me feel good."

"I wish I could say I'm surprised," I sighed again. "Look, I'm sorry about my brother. He was... *is* a giant dick. Maybe he'll get a personality transplant and be nicer some day." I chuckled awkwardly, but I wanted to burst out in laughter.

Because that's exactly what had happened. Not that she could know that. Based on her smell, she was completely human.

"Well, maybe if he just cut back on the drugs and alcohol he'd be a better lay." She shrugged. "To be honest, he was kind of boring."

I blinked for a second. "Wait. He was doing drugs and alcohol... while having sex with you?" I knew we'd found way too many bottles of tequila and a couple of bottles of pills in his room. I just hadn't expected that he was doing them... during sex.

"Yeah, on Monday night." She shrugged again. "I think he'd been drinking before I even showed up. We'd barely made out for a minute before he said it wasn't working for him. The douche. He popped a viagra then made me change positions. It was only later that I realized he'd moved me so that he could see himself."

"He had both tequila *and* viagra while you were with him?" Well, no wonder his heart stopped. If he'd had one of the ecstasy we'd found…

"Yeah." Then a little laugh came out of her. "Not that it did him any good. No offense, dude, but your brother isn't that great in bed. Sure he's big enough, but he's… well, like I said, boring. The mirror was the most interesting thing he did. But it was only about him watching himself."

"I'm sorry," I said. "Really. Feel free to steer clear of him." Grayson wouldn't be happy if Jonathan's conquests came after him. "And, uh, anyone else that you know he's slept with in the past. Yesterday was a hard day for him. I have hopes that he'll be nicer."

When a cruel laugh came from her, I grinned.

"Or at least not as much of an asshole," I conceded.

"Alright," she smiled. "I'm Katrina, by the way."

"Jackson." I stuck out my hand for her to shake. She held it longer than necessary.

"Jackson." She looked up at me through her lashes. "So how much do you look like your brother… other than the hair?" Her eyes glanced down to my crotch. Ugh.

"Well," I pasted on a smile. "We are twins. But my boyfriend gets a little too jealous if he has to share me with anyone."

"Oh." Her face fell. Then she also put a fake smile on her face. "Well, he's one lucky guy. It was nice meeting you, Jackson. Hopefully I never run into you or your brother ever again!"

I laughed. "You too, Katrina. Thanks for letting me know about the other night."

She shrugged as she turned and walked out the door. "No problem!"

Well, damn. Now I knew why Jonathan had been stumbling around in no clothes. Why he'd collapsed. I'd bet everything I had that his heart gave up on him between the tequila, viagra, and ecstasy.

Fucking idiot.

22

CARY CARPENTER

My Vampire Boyfriend: I just talked to Jonathan's fuck from Monday night. Sweet girl. But she definitely shed some light on his death.

Me: *What'd she say?*

My Vampire Boyfriend: That he'd definitely had tequila and viagra while she was there. I suspect he had some X after she left.

Me: *Shit. Did she say if he was any good at least?*

My Vampire Boyfriend: Perv. She said he was boring. LOL. Apparently she didn't appreciate him staring at himself in the mirror while he fucked her.

Me: *Oh, god. He didn't.*

My Vampire Boyfriend: What do you think?

Me: *Poor girl.*

My Vampire Boyfriend: Yeah. Anyway. That'd explain the boner Grayson showed up with. And why he hadn't been able to feel the cold.

Me: *Yep. We should let Grayson know. Though, I think he purged all of that out of him.*

My Vampire Boyfriend: It was a rough night. I gotta get to class now. I'm a bit late since I stopped to talk to her.

Me: *Have fun!*

As I slipped my phone back in my pocket, I felt a cold wave of lust wash over me.

It wasn't normal incubus magic. Instead of the heat that I was used to, this was icy. Frigid.

Dread came heady with the lust.

I shivered and looked around me.

Almost immediately I saw who I suspected it was coming from. A petite yet curvy woman with a wild mane of black hair was talking to a male student near the door of the fine arts building.

Suddenly the lust radiating off of her didn't just feel cold, it felt destructive.

Hateful. Slimy.

I shivered and pulled my phone back out.

When we'd packed up Jonathan's and Grayson's rooms, Gray had grabbed his phone, and we'd added him to our group chat.

Me: What does that teacher look like? The one that tried to kill you?

Zombie: Very curly black hair. Kinda crazy. Big boobs.

Precious Prescilla: About my height. Dark skin and eyes. Beautiful, but in a creepy way.

Me: Got it. I think I've found her. I'm going to follow her for a bit.

Kitty Kat: Be careful. We don't want her attention on you if she tried to kill Grayson.

My Vampire Boyfriend: I don't think there's any doubt she tried to kill him. We just need evidence. But, yes, please be careful, Cary.

Me: Will do.

Precious Prescilla: I'd really rather you NOT follow her. She's not safe.

Zombie: Agreed. The woman is seriously crazy.

Me: I'll be careful. I promise.

I put the phone away and looked around for something that was a logical reason why I might stick around this area and then follow her when she left.

I'd be missing my class today, but it would be worth it if I could get any evidence that she'd tried to kill Grayson.

Before I could find some sort of cover, though, she turned and went into the fine arts building.

I followed.

If nothing else, I knew they treated the hallways like a student art gallery.

I could always claim I was just looking at paintings instead of stalking a psychopath.

23
PRESCILLA BENNETT

I gripped my backpack tighter, steeling my spine to walk into art.

I took several deep breaths.

I could do this.

It was just one class. And we weren't really sure that Ms. Gamal had been the one to kill Grayson.

Yeah.

Right.

We knew it was her. We just needed evidence.

And then my racing heart calmed as I thought about the fact that Cary was trailing her. Maybe he'd stick around near the studio for today's class.

Before I could pull my phone back out to ask him to do exactly that, a warm arm came around my waist from behind me. Cradling me.

I looked up right into Jonathan's dark eyes.

At once, my tense muscles loosened, and a sigh escaped. "Gra– er… Jay. What are you doing here?"

"I just came from my meeting with the academic counselor."

"How'd that go?" I turned so that I could look up at him, but he didn't let me out of his arms.

Not that I minded one single bit.

"Well, *I* was definitely not keeping *my* grades up. I now have three more years instead of just this one. And I am no longer an accounting major. I used the excuse of not making A's in the math classes."

"Why am I not surprised?" I asked dryly.

"Anyway, with some rearranging of things, I'll be able to get an art history degree. Apparently *I* actually liked history because I had pretty good grades in an excessive number of history classes. But it means I now need to focus on taking a bunch of art classes over again since I haven't taken them."

"Oh. That's… good?"

"I made sure I got placed in this class with you. I don't want you here with her alone." He gave me a wink.

"Thank you… Jay," I buried my face into his chest. I still wasn't used to how much larger he was now. Grayson hadn't been short in his old body. But he'd been lean. Now, in Jonathan's body, he was all large slabs of muscle.

I jumped back at the sharp voice that filled the studio.

"Good morning, lovely people. Let's begin!"

The two of us jumped apart and spun around when we heard Ms. Gamal.

I knew the moment she realized who was standing next to me. Who was *really* standing next to me. Her eyes narrowed and a low hiss came from her.

"We have much to cover today," she gritted through her clenched teeth. "Have a seat."

Grayson followed me toward my normal space, and, with one look at the girl next to me, claimed that spot. She scrambled to an empty easel on the other side of the room. It was probably safer for her over there, anyway. Away from us.

Because right now, nowhere felt safe.

Especially if Amy Gamal was in the room.

24

GRAYSON LEBLANC

You know that saying about a watched pot never boils? Try watching the clock tick down the minutes left in a class.

At seven minutes until the end, Ms. Gamal announced that everyone did such a lovely job, she'd end class a little early today.

I could already tell that she wouldn't be letting the two of us out of here without a few words.

I could also tell by the way she seethed at me, she clearly knew that I had body jumped.

Nothing like discovering that your art skills really do rely on the ability of the body to manipulate the tools… and then following that disappointing revelation by having to confront your would-be-killer.

Although, I supposed she actually did kill me. I was only here thanks to my mother's voodoo charm.

So yeah, killer.

The more I thought about it all, the angrier I got. And the angrier I got, the more I thought that this confrontation was a pretty fucking good idea.

Prescilla stood slightly behind me, and when the last student trickled out, Ms. Gamal shut the door and locked it.

That was... confident. A tad presumptuous.

I opened my mouth, ready to accuse her. Ready to hurl insults. Ready to say... so fucking much to this bitch. But I didn't get a chance.

She moved in front of me inhumanly fast and then–

Well I really didn't know how to explain what happened next. Somehow she ejected me from my new body. It flopped to the floor, and Prescilla screamed.

I tried to reassure her that I was okay. That I still stood right here. But after a few failed attempts, it became painfully clear that she couldn't hear me.

Ms. Gamal began to talk, but in my noncorporeal state, her voice sounded like it echoed down a long hallway.

"I can't believe this sniveling twat survived." She sent a kick right to the abdomen of my body.

Prescilla sobbed and clutched my body closer. "No! Don't touch him. You've done enough damage."

She laughed, but it sounded cold and humorless.

"Oh that useless boy isn't quite dead yet, you pathetic girl." She whirled around, her face mere inches away from mine... and she purred. "Isn't that right, Grayson my sweet?"

"You can see me?"

"He's not dead?" Prescilla looked down at the lifeless body still clutched to her chest.

"Of course I can see you. A goddess's power is limitless." She ran a finger down my cheek, and I nearly felt it. "At least, it would be if my beloved weren't so ruthless with his punishments." She smirked a little, but I could barely keep up with the conversation.

Instead of trying to make sense of her ramblings, I tried to move towards my body, but it felt like swimming through sludge. I didn't get far before Ms. Gamal stepped in front of me.

"Now, now, Grayson. I can't have you hopping back into that meat sack just yet."

"What do you want from me?!"

She blinked, and her eyes shifted to a light green with tiny slitted pupils. When she blinked again they were normal, but her shrieking proved that she was far from under control.

"What I WANTED was to give you a gift!" She took a breath before continuing on in her normal detached calm. "You denied my gift. You *do not* deny a gift from a goddess without consequences, my dear boy."

She'd already killed me, what else could she possibly do?

The bitch walked back to Prescilla and hooked her nasty fingers under Prescilla's, forcing my girl to look into that monster's eyes. "And this one... she is worthy. She is not quite like these humans. She is *more* and she will be mine."

I kept pushing myself forward, but I seemed to be only moving a few inches at a time.

"It's time for you to wake up, my dear." With her other hand, Ms. Gamal tapped the very center of Prescilla's temple.

I was so close to my body. So fucking close.

Prescilla's eyes rolled back into her head, and she fell asleep.

So close to my body I could almost touch it...

Just.

A little.

Further.

25

AMY GAMAL

I no sooner got Prescilla lying down when that asshole Grayson popped back up in that body he stole with an annoying gasp.

My hand shot out and grabbed ahold of his neck.

I shouldn't be forced to deal with this asshole. Yet again.

"So tell me, Grayson, how *did* you manage to swoop into another body?" I leaned closer and took a deep inhale. "It smells like an upgrade for sure. Tired of the dhampir life? Gonna try fang-banging instead?"

I threw my head back and laughed.

My hold stayed firm, but not too tight. He still managed to wheeze out words. "What did you do to Prescilla?"

I leaned in very close. Willing him to see the fierce dedication in my eyes.

"I'm waking her up."

I released his neck and shoved him back with a show of force. He slid across the length of the studio, crashing into easels and stools.

I stood and tilted my chin slightly. Showing him with my own dismissive body language that he was a lesser being.

"You had your chance, Grayson. You would have had so much more than you could have hoped for in this pathetic little life of yours. But you fucked that up." I studied my fingers for a moment. Wishing with all my might for my hand to change. Just a slight alteration. I longed for fur again.

I reached down and tucked a braid behind Prescilla's ear.

"Once my Nubian queen wakes up, there will be nothing keeping her from me."

I stood and walked to the door of the studio. Unlocked it.

But I stopped myself from opening the door.

I looked back just as Grayson returned to Prescilla's side.

Partially because I couldn't help taking one more jab, and partially because I loved a flair for the dramatic, I made my last words count.

"I may not have taken your life completely the first time, but I will take your heart this time."

I smiled as I left the room.

26
GUILLERMO PÉREZ

I had just set down my bookbag and was about to make a snack, when Grayson came flying through the front door of the house like a bat out of hell.

"Help!"

The panic in Grayson's plea had me in front of him in seconds.

My jaguar practically ripped Prescilla's body from Grayson's arms and snarled. A rage I had never felt before began to surge through me. The fact that I now held my mate and that her breathing and heartbeat sounded normal was the only thing preventing me from ripping the guy to shreds.

"Explain." I managed to grit the one word command out between my grinding teeth.

"Woah," he held his hands in front of him. As if the gesture would placate me. Or stop my jaguar. "I didn't do anything. This was not me. It was that crazy murderous bitch!"

I took a deep breath and consoled my inner beast by sniffing my mate.

She seemed… fine.

Then what the hell was going on? Crazy murderous bitch?

"You mean that art professor that was hitting on Prescilla?" I tried to sift through the information they'd shared about this woman, but I didn't have much to go on.

I wished I had a face to direct my hate towards.

"Yeah, and me. And you know, the one that actually murdered me?" He sounded exhausted, and I knew that he was angry, but right now I didn't really care.

Before I got a chance to demand any more answers, Jack gently pushed his way into the house.

"Hey guys, what's—" When he saw my mate in my arms, he rushed towards me.

Not a smart move.

My body reacted on instinct. I punched out as Jack drew close and the force of it sent him flying across the room.

I took a few steps back, curling around my mate's body and clutching her tightly in my arms.

She's *mine*. They couldn't take her.

I snarled at the other males in the room. Almost daring them to come near me again.

Labored breathing reached the front door— which still hung wide open, and a hand slapped against the door frame.

"Fucking hell zombie man! You can... move fast... when you need to."

Cary bent over at the waist and took deep pulls of air into his lungs.

When he stood back up and surveyed the room around him, he winced.

"Alright then." He stepped inside and gently closed the door behind him, before wrapping an arm around Grayson's shoulder and directing him to the large chair in the living room. The one farthest from me.

Jack stood up in a deliberately slow movement. He glared at me with his red eyes and hissed through his exposed fangs.

"Jack, love... how about we all calm down. Come sit with me." Cary's tone remained calm, but there was clear worry in his eyes.

"As soon as *he* explains what he did to Prescilla." Jack's hard glare relaxed just a tiny bit when Cary touched his chest.

"He didn't do it. Look at me, love." Cary waited for Jack to comply. "He didn't do anything."

Jack relaxed and rested his head against Cary's as he breathed deeply.

"I'm okay." Jack whispered.

Cary kissed him on the forehead. "Good. now why don't you have a seat over here and we can all figure out what is going on."

Jack nodded, and they moved to the loveseat. Jack plopped down on the cushions and eyed me suspiciously, but Cary just leaned against the arm rest and scrubbed his hands down his face a few times.

When he pulled his hands away, his eyes met mine and shone with a calm understanding.

"Now I'm not going to ask you to come over here big guy, because I know you can't right now. You just hold on to your mate and listen to her heartbeat. You know she is okay." He nodded at me, and I gulped.

The man part of me felt ashamed for my reactions to my friends. But my jaguar was doing what he knew best. Protecting his mate.

I only hoped the guys wouldn't hold a grudge.

When I glanced over at Grayson, I saw how stiff his body was. And his eyes shone with unshed tears.

Cary broke the silence again. Almost like he was the only one who could keep a level head. "So, I know that you and Prescilla came out of the classroom way after class had ended. I was doing a little digging in the professor's office when I saw you. All I found in there were a bunch of weird coded notes."

"She locked us in after class and..." Grayson paused and shook his head. "She expelled me from my body! Then she did something to Prescilla to knock her out."

"She what?" Jackson and I yelled at the same time. I turned a glare on him.

"She kicked you out of Jonathan's body?" Jackson ignored me.

"How'd she knock PB out?" I asked.

"Yes," Grayson nodded. "And she could still see and hear me, even when I wasn't in the body."

"Interesting," Cary mused.

"I have no idea what she did to Prescilla." Grayson shrugged. "She tapped her on the forehead and Prescilla just crumpled."

"That wasn't a normal tap." Sure, the statement was obvious, but I felt like it needed to be reinforced. The witch had done something to *my mate*.

"No it wasn't," Grayson agreed. "The murdering slime said something about the Nubian Queen joining her? I honestly didn't understand half of what she said because I was freaking out that Prescilla had gone down so fast."

I looked down at my mate. She looked almost like she was sleeping. I trailed my finger across her cheek and brushed a few locks away from her face.

I hadn't expected for her to flutter her gorgeous eyelashes and look up at me with a smile as if nothing at all had happened.

"Hey there, handsome. Mind telling me where I am and who you are?"

To be fair, though... I hadn't expected her to not recognize me either.

27
PRESCILLA BENNET

I looked around in confusion. This... was not my home.
Rather than a village filled with gardens surrounding each warm hut, I was inside some sort of building that looked... cold. Stale.

And I was not surrounded by my people. I had no idea who these men were, but they were not mine. Granted, the one holding me was as sexy as sexy could be. Part of me wanted to curl up in his arms and never move. But...

I looked at the one that seemed the most calm. He was pale with a light hair color. Fear flooded my system.

Romans.

Oh gods, no!

I jumped up, pulling away from the man cradling me.

"I do not care what you want. You will not take me and my people!" I reached for an arrow with one hand and my bow with the other. But I quickly learned that neither were on my back where they should have been.

I looked down at the items covering my body and shuddered. This material was coarse. And way too close to my skin. How was I supposed to move and fight in these garments?

"Where are my weapons?" I asked the man that had been holding me. The one whose inner animal called to me.

His brow wrinkled. "You don't have any weapons? Though, your phone fell out of your pocket..." He stooped and picked a flat rectangle of... some sort... off the floor then tried to hand it to me.

"I do not know what that is." I spun toward the other men in the room, looking them over again. Trying to figure out just who they were.

The two that were not pale were tall with markings painted all over their skin.

And they were *large*.

So very large.

They must be some of those barbarian mercenaries the Romans were known for hiring sometimes.

How had I been captured by the enemy? Why were they all standing here so calmly if so?

Trust Cary to be calm no matter what was going on. He always seemed to ride out whatever storm had blown in.

"Why're you always so damn calm, Cary?" I asked.

His eyes lit up. "You know who I am?"

"Of course," I scoffed. "Why wouldn't I know you?"

"Well," he hesitated then exchanged glances with Jackson. "Because you don't taste like you. Not all the way at least. I'm getting a lot of... someone else."

"Why are you tasting me?" I shook my head. That wasn't really important right now.

I searched for a doorway, some way to get out of here. Away from my capturers. Away from the man I felt drawn to. The man I wanted to lick from head to toe.

Stop.

Focus.

You cannot save your people if you are drooling over a man.

Even if he worked my body in the most delicious ways last night...

I shook my head to try and dislodge those thoughts. They didn't all feel like *mine*.

"Where am I?" I asked again. I tried to make it sound like an innocent question, but I desperately wanted to know so that I could get out of here.

"Prescilla," one of the big ones said while reaching out a hand toward me. "How about you come sit down, and we'll talk about this."

"Who is Prescilla?" I asked. I did not take his hand, though it was large and strong and looked like it would be very excellent at... pleasuring me. I crossed my arms to stop myself from reaching out to him.

They all exchanged glances, worry creasing their brows. Confusion filling their eyes.

Well, I was worried and confused too. How had I gotten here?

"I do not have time for this," I muttered. I started moving, heading toward the large opening in the wall, where light spilled in.

"Where are you going?" One of the big ones asked.

"To find my people." I pulled back the cloth over the opening in the wall and took a step forward. But something solid stopped me. "What witchcraft is this?" I slammed my hand in the air, meeting a cool but solid barrier.

"It's a window?" The shifter said. Gods, he smelled so good. "If you want to leave, try the door." He gestured to a dark gray rectangle in the wall with a round ball protruding from it.

"Meemo? How does the bond feel?" Cary asked.

Meemo shrugged. "Her emotions are all over the place. But at least the bond itself is strong. So whoever this is... they're bonded to me too?"

I spun back toward my bonded. "Where is this door you speak of? I see no door!"

I blinked and realized I was standing in front of it.

Duh. You're such an idiot, Prescilla.

I reached towards the knob with my head held high, and threw it open, leaving the cold house and the sexy males behind.

I might not be in my lands.
I might not be in my own robes and fighting armor.
I might not have my weapons.
I might not know what these people wanted.
But I was still a *queen*.
And I would protect my people… no matter what.

28
JACKSON MILLER

"What. The. Hell?" I looked at Cary and Grayson, totally fucking confused and–frankly?–a little pissed. "Why'd you remind her about the door, Meemo?"

"She was going to break the window," he shrugged. "Come on, let's just follow her and make sure she's safe. I don't want to leave my mate alone."

"I'm not entirely sure that's your mate, though, even if your bond is in place." Cary said slowly. "The energy coming off her isn't totally Prescilla. It's... more animalistic. She doesn't taste right."

"Are you saying someone else is in Prescilla's body now?" Grayson's fists were clenching and unclenching at his sides. "It's not bad enough she threw me out of the body I've taken over... She threw Prescilla out of her body and put someone *else* in it?!"

Meemo growled and prowled out the door. "I'm following her. Come or don't. But I'm not leaving her side."

We all followed him out, though Cary stopped long enough to lock up the house behind us.

"So now we've got to figure out who it is riding Prescilla's body," I said. "And how to get her back."

"Before she hurts anyone while trying to save... her people?" Cary mused as he threw an arm around me. "Is she some kind of leader?"

"She certainly looked like a queen," Grayson said. After a moment, his lips quirked up. "But then, I always thought of her as *my* queen, so that's really nothing new."

"Does anyone else feel a weird pull toward her?" I asked. When they all just stared back at me, I clarified. "I mean, more than the pull we've been feeling the last couple of weeks. Ever since she woke up, it feels like my vampire side just has to be with her."

"Yes," Cary nodded. "But it doesn't feel... right? Like my incubus wanted her before, but now it's almost like he's being forced to want her now."

"That's it," Grayson said. "Like I have no choice but to be with her. When before I just *wanted* to be with her."

"Yes," Meemo growled. But then he didn't continue on.

"Where are we going?" Grayson suddenly pulled to a stop.

"Wherever she is," Cary waved to Prescilla on the sidewalk ahead of us.

"She's headed straight for the art building," Grayson said. Dread and horror filled his voice. "She's going straight for my murderer."

"No," Meemo growled. He broke into a run, trying to get to Prescilla before she entered the building.

But he was too late because she was already pulling the door open to enter the dim building.

"Cary," I grabbed his arm. "Please. I know you don't like to use your magic to influence people to do things. But I think you might be the only one of us that can get through to her."

"I'm not going to force her to come with us," Cary curled his lip.

I knew how he felt about doing that.

I knew what I was asking him to do. And that it may be too much.

I shook my head. I didn't like the idea any more than he did..

"I'm just saying if she won't listen to us, you might need to try to… direct her back to us. For her own safety."

"Hurry," Grayson interrupted us. "I don't want her in there alone." He held open the front door of the art building, and we both ran to catch up to him.

Entering the darkness of the campus building suddenly felt like being swallowed whole in a giant maw.

I shuddered at the thought as I crossed the threshold.

Hold on, Prescilla.

We're coming for you.

29
CARY CARPENTER

We followed Prescilla through the halls to the part of the building where the administrative offices were. I wasn't sure where she was headed, but every step she took made my heart sink a little more.

When Prescilla threw open an office door, I groaned. I knew *exactly* whose office that was. "Guys…"

Prescilla draped herself in the door like she was posing for a sexy photo shoot or something. Where the hell had this person come from that took over our precious Prescilla's body?

I wanted our sweet girl back, dammit!

"Hello, my goddess," Prescilla purred.

While Meemo and Grayson growled in stereo, I paid attention to the lust rolling off of Prescilla… and Ms. Gamal. It felt like they were feeding each other. Building the wave of lust. Amplifying the signal.

Almost against my will, I moved to get closer to Prescilla. I needed to be beside her. To guard my queen.

"What the hell?" Jackson hissed at me. "Cary, hit her with your magic."

I shook my head as I came to stand next to Prescilla. "Hello, Amy," I also purred.

Again, growling. But this time from Jackson. I didn't let my smile loose. I needed to play this just right if I were going to succeed.

Ms. Gamal looked up from her desk where she was throwing things into a suitcase.

What the fuck? Was she leaving?

When her eyes landed on me, a crocodile smile slid across her face. I tried my best not to shudder at the wicked gleam in her eyes. At the way she so obviously wanted to eat me alive.

"Hello, little lover," Ms. Gamal crooned. "I've been waiting ever so long for you to return to me."

"You woke me up," Prescilla said with a note of accusation in her voice.

"Of course I did," Ms. Gamal preened. "I was so shocked to find you here, hiding in this backwater town. Buried under layers of..." she curled her lip up in disgust, "innocence. I had to set you free."

"Mmm," Prescilla hummed.

She was rubbing a hand up and down the door frame. Stroking it. Like it was her lover.

Suddenly I really, really didn't like Jackson's idea to use my incubus magic on her. If she was acting like this without me pumping pheromones into the room, how bad would it be if I did?

I saw a flash of triumph in Ms. Gamal's eyes, and that sealed my decision.

Without moving a single muscle, I concentrated on the well of magic inside me and sent it questing out into the room.

As soon as a tendril wrapped around Prescilla, I whispered a compulsion into her mind. *Go. Now. Stay with Meemo and forget Amy.*

She jerked her head around, eyes searching. Then she found Meemo in the hallway behind me. She immediately slunk toward him, swinging her hips.

I moved my focus back to the real enemy here.

Another tendril of my magic wrapped around Ms. Gamal. Not wanting to take any chances, I waited until several of the vine-like magic had encompassed her. Then I pulled them tight and sank a suggestion into her mind. *Go. Now. Leave this place and never come back. Forget you ever saw Prescilla or Grayson.*

Then she did something no one else had ever done.

She writhed in my magic for a bit. Like she was trying to hump it, or something.

Moaning seductively.

Before she snarled. Her lips pulled back from her teeth and a roar burst from her chest.

"Incubus!"

Never had a word been so filled with belittlement. Disgust. Condescension. Dismissal.

What the fuck was happening right now?

"Fucking incubus," she snarled. "You think you can lust me? Work your little baby magic on me? I am the Devourer. A goddess more ancient than you can imagine. But more, I *am* sex personified. Your power doesn't work on me. You're no match for me! You are nothing."

A cold chill raced down my spine. Only one response came to mind.

Run!

I spun around to find an orgy happening in the hall behind me.

Meemo and Grayson had Prescilla crushed between the two of them. She and Meemo were devouring each other's faces while Grayson was biting down hard on her neck.

Jackson was... damn. My boyfriend was standing next to the trio, hungrily watching them. With his dick in his hand. Wanking away.

Maybe I'd pushed a little too much of my incubus magic into the air.

I shoved at them all, trying to break them apart. "Come on! Get out of here!" I yelled at them.

When they all looked at me with glazed over eyes, I screamed, "Run!"

But they all just blinked owlishly at me.

Damnit, Cary.

Why did I have to be so damn sexy…

30
PRESCILLA BENNETT

The bonded one tasted so very delicious. I wasn't sure exactly what his animal was, but I knew it was some kind of big cat.

Really, though, what his animal may be didn't matter. What mattered was that he was a strong warrior, and he was *mine*.

One of the blood demons was at my back, feasting on my neck. While I might never have chosen one of the creatures for my own, I couldn't deny the fact that his fangs sinking into me gave me much pleasure.

I writhed between the two, desperate to mate. To bring forth the next generation of warriors. To make my people strong.

"Holy fucking hell!"

I slowly turned my face in the direction of the yell and was astonished to see the Roman there, mouth hanging open, shoving at us.

"Snap out of it, guys! She's coming for us!"

The mercenary that had been standing next to us, taking pleasure in ours, snapped straight up. His eyes widened as he looked behind the Roman. "Run!" he screamed.

In a slow haze of lust, I turned to see what had him panicking.

From Amy's office a… beast was emerging. Tall. Massively broad. Lion… but not. Crocodile… but not. What the hell?

"Meemo! We gotta go!" I pushed my boyfriend off of me and grabbed Grayson's wrist. "Come on!"

I started running for the exits to the… why the heck were we in the art building? It didn't matter. Getting away from the monster did.

"What the hell is that thing?" Grayson asked as he wiped blood off of his mouth.

"No idea, but it's not going to get my girl!" Meemo yelled.

As we all turned a corner down another hallway, Meemo stopped and looked back down the one we'd just come from.

"You can't have her!" He roared.

We all skidded to a stop, staring at Meemo.

"What the hell, man?" Jackson asked.

"Don't you see?" Meemo shouted, waving at it. "It's only interested in PB! We have to stop it!"

Oh, my sexy, sexy guard. A purr rumbled up from my throat. I couldn't stop myself from reaching out and wrapping my arms around him, pulling him toward me.

"Do not fear the demon," I kissed up his neck. "I've trained my army very well." I bit gently into his ear.

The cat shivered in my hold, but then looked toward my other capturers. "You have to stop that thing from getting to PB."

"My strong, sexy guard," I purred as I rubbed against his hip. "I shall reward you greatly for slaying the beast for me."

"I can't decide if that totally turns me on… or completely grosses me out," the one that'd been biting my neck said. Such a sexy blood demon.

"I'm going to go with *greatly disturbing*," the other blood demon whispered.

Then the beast rounded around the corner, and her eyes zeroed in on me.

The amount of conflicting emotions warring inside of me felt overwhelming.

Half of me felt aroused, powerful, and in charge.
The other half?
She was fucking scared shitless.
What had I gotten myself into now?

31
GRAYSON LEBLANC

I had never drunk blood like that before. As a dhampir, I didn't actually drink blood. I just ate my steak a bit... Well, okay; it was raw. But I never actually had fangs.

It had been a little cooler than I expected. And oh, so good.

But right now the monster was coming at us. Again.

"Don't let her go!" I realized that was probably a stupid thing to say to the guy who was *actually* her mate, but I couldn't take the words back now.

Instead of saying something dickhead-ish, he just quirked an eyebrow at me.

He was a far classier guy than me, that's for sure.

If I were being honest with myself, I did kind of like him.

But I didn't plan on admitting that out loud any time soon. Not when I still wanted so badly to smash Prescilla's petite little body between us again.

"We're going to have to rush this thing. Grayson, go after the left side legs, and I will go right. Cary, use those sexy long legs of yours and straddle that muzzle."

Jack's voice snapped me back to the present.

Right. Crazy chimera monster thingy came at us.

I couldn't help the nagging feeling at the back of my head that I'd seen this thing before.

Before I could come up with the answer, everyone began to move.

Jack rushed forward, and I jumped into action. I pushed this large body faster than I ever could my old one and slammed it right into the legs of the beast. It toppled to the right, and Jack just barely missed getting squashed.

Oops.

Guess I didn't know my new strength yet.

"Sorry!" I yelled over to him.

He took the opportunity to grab onto the beast's front legs, and I took that as my cue to secure the back legs.

Cary jumped on the head a mere seconds before the snappy fucker could latch onto Jack's mid-section.

Alright…

Now what?

So normally, when a predator got trapped, it would begin to lash out. It was the reaction one would expect. Flailing, thrashing, snarling, anything like that. Those are the types of reactions that we were all bracing for.

Did you know what we weren't bracing for?

Inhuman moaning.

Not like disembodied, ghostly sounds.

Oh, no. That would be creepy, but at least it could be a ploy to convince us it was in pain or something and try to trick us to let down our guard out of pity.

No, this moan was far more disturbing.

It was like a woman who was fast approaching her sexual peak.

I curled my lip in disgust, and when I glanced at Cary, he looked like he was about to toss his cookies.

Then… the fucking thing began to shrink down.

So it shrank down into a naked woman while I had its left leg, and Jack has its right arm, and Cary— well, he jumped the fuck away so he didn't end up with his balls in her face.

Once she was fully human again, the bitch started laughing.

She reached up and snatched the collar of my shirt. Pulling me closer.

"You can't stop me. I *will* eat your heart, boy." She released her grip and moaned again. This time arching her back.

"My love calls for me." A smile far too wide for her human face was the last thing we saw before she disappeared.

No, I didn't mean she overpowered us and ran. I mean one minute she was there and the next, she dissipated like a mist.

I only had two thoughts racing through my head right then.

The first one–

"What the actual fuck just happened?!" Cary seemed to share that thought.

And the other–

"I don't know, but at least the bitch is gone." And Jack had that thought as well.

Maybe I wasn't so different from them after all.

I didn't know if I liked the idea, or if I was terrified of it, but if it kept me with Prescilla, then I would just have to get used to them.

When I looked at Cary, he shot me a saucy wink.

I rolled my eyes at him, but a small part of me liked it.

A small, *tiny* part of me might just have been harboring the idea that I might actually want to kiss the sexy bastard.

Where the fuck were these new thoughts and ideas coming from exactly?

I blamed the new body.

32
GUILLERMO PÉREZ

Whoever her 'love' was, had perfect timing. While her sudden disappearance was jarring, I guess it kind of fit. She seemed like the type to get bored easily.

She had kept calling herself a goddess, after all.

How long could a goddess possibly remain happily occupied in a college?

I also assumed that PB would go back to her normal, wonderful self.

I was so very wrong.

As the guys began walking back towards us, Prescilla began to throw her elbows back into me. Were I a human, that would have hurt. Thankfully my shifter abs came in handy.

"No! You can't leave me here!" The sound of her anguish at the disappearance of the former art professor felt like a knife in the gut.

"It will be okay." I attempted to calm her, but my voice sounded too flat and void of emotion.

I just wanted my mate back.

"Okay? Are you a complete moron? Nothing about this is okay! I shouldn't be here. I don't want to be here! That hateful lizard doesn't get to just wake me and then leave!" I had never heard Prescilla's voice so angry before, but what my ears heard most... was desperation.

If that were true, then this may not be a permanent situation...

"Where did you idiots send her? No. It doesn't matter. Bring her back this instant. I will not be left in this plane. I am a Queen, and I *earned* my right to rest peacefully!" Her words tore at my heart.

So, this was simply a long descendant of the Nubian Queen, and that goddess pulled her into PB's body. But why?

And how did we get PB back?

I looked around at the guys. Hoping one of them had an idea.

Grayson looked just as worried as I felt. Jack looked pissed, but I think he just had a permanent scowl. Unless he was still angry at me for punching him across the room?

Then there was Cary. He always seemed to be our logical thinker. The planner.

He looked up at me and nodded. "Meemo, if anyone can bring her back, it's going to be her mate. Use the bond." He tried for a calm tone, but I could hear the little bit of worry he tried to hide.

I didn't like it.

I never wanted my mate to feel forced.

But... dammit!

I didn't have a better idea.

I let out a sigh as I tried to turn her around in my arms, but she wiggled hard. Fighting me. I couldn't do this alone.

I looked up into Grayson's eyes. This was it.

I had to be the one to make the choice. I had to be the strong one.

I had to push the three of us across that threshold that my love had been trying so hard to dance around. I just hoped she didn't hate me for making the choice for her. For all of us.

"Help me. Help *her*. She needs a distraction. Make it a *good* one."

He nodded and licked his lips, moving towards us and grasping PB's arms just above my own hands.

We worked together to turn my half-crazed mate around. He moved his hands to cup her cheeks and pressed his lips softly against hers. She continued to fight for a brief moment, before sinking into the moment.

When I released her arms, she wrapped them around Grayson and pulled his body flush against her own. They moaned together at the contact.

Seeing them like this… Hearing them like this…

I thought I would be hurt. Jealous. Something much more negative.

Instead I felt instantly warm, and my dick went fucking rock hard.

I pulled PB's shirt away from her shoulder and exposed the still raw mating mark.

I would never do this twice in a row to her. It would be more pain than pleasure this time. But I *had* to try.

I relaxed my jaw, letting my jaguar's teeth distend, and sank them quickly into her flesh. Refused to give myself a second to change my mind.

She bucked and moaned, but the moans turned into a whimper. The sound was a clear mix of pleasure and pain.

I released my hold and licked the tiny tendrils of blood, before straightening her shirt.

Grayson pulled back, and they both stood there panting.

"What… the hell… happened to me?"

She sounded like herself again, but I turned to Cary, not willing to get my hopes up yet.

He smiled. "She certainly tastes like our Prescilla again. Just a tad bit spicier. And uh.." He stopped and licked his lips. "It's calling to me… *a lot*."

I turned her around to face me and smashed my lips to hers.

Finally, I let the relief wash through me.

33
PRESCILLA BENNETT

The guys promised that we would hash everything out, once we got back to the house.

Apparently, we ended up in the art building at school.

On a Wednesday night.

Nope, not weird at all.

You know what else was totally not weird?

All four of the guys sporting massive boners.

Like seriously. It made my nipples hard and tingly, and my mouth began to water. Imagining all those dicks on me, in me. Using me. Making me scream and writhe in pleasure.

If the pant tents were any indication, they were all packing very nice weapons like my delicious mate.

A quick vision fluttered into my mind. My body grinding against Meemo while Grayson dry humped my ass, biting me with his fangs. Jack standing beside us. Biting that grumpy lip and stroking his big cock.

Was that… real?

But then all the pain started to set in, and suddenly… I didn't give a fuck about anyone's hard-on.

I had a killer headache, my shoulder blade was on fire, and my vagina?

"Why do my lady lips feel like I've been ripped apart?" I quickly covered my mouth. I had not meant for that to come blurting out of me like that.

The guys all froze and then turned in unison to stare at Meemo, who blushed and yet looked ridiculously proud all at once.

Oh... Yeah.

I guess losing my virginity to a guy that big would do it.

I paused with my hand on the exit door and threw my head back and laughed. It didn't take long before the guys joined me.

It was clear that some crazy shit went down tonight, so I figured we were all due a good laugh.

Once we got ourselves under control, Meemo pressed against me on the right side. Then, in a shocking turn of events, Grayson pressed against my left.

When I looked into his eyes they were full of adoration and playfulness. There he was. There was my Grayson. I didn't hold back on my urges, and quickly pressed a peck to his cheek.

I felt sure one of the explanations for tonight would include all the sexual tension and the interesting position I was in when I... woke up? Sandwiched between Meemo and Gray was something I would definitely like to understand.

And... if possible... repeat.

When the guys pushed open the doors, I expected to see an eerily empty campus green stretched in front of us.

That was definitely *not* the case.

Instead, the green was positively full of people. Men and women. All coming towards us.

And some of them looked far less than human.

Some of them were only partially dressed.

There were even a large chunk of them completely naked.

They all had two things in common.

One, they looked horny as hell.

And two, they were looking right at me, like I was a snack and they were starving.

"Uh, guys. It looks like an explanation may need to come a little faster than waiting until we get back home." I tried really hard not to let the panic fill my voice, but I couldn't help it. Today had been all sorts of fucked.

When I woke up this morning, I was naked on a blanket in the woods with my jaguar shifter mate. I was still holding on to a tiny bit of fear that Grayson's body jumping was some kind of sign for the zombie apocalypse.

Instead of the dead rising... we had dicks rising.

While I wanted to be flattered, I had never been the kind of girl that found bed hopping interesting.

Not shaming those who did. You do you, girl. But it just wasn't something for me.

And while I could appreciate the attractiveness of a fellow female, I had never gotten a lady boner for one. Art professor excluded, because I wasn't totally convinced that had been a natural reaction.

So all this sex oozing towards me from about one hundred of my fellow classmates did *not* have me excited.

So instead of a zombie apocalypse, I now faced a... hornypocalypse?

"I really want to joke about being too sexy for my own good, but there is no way this is normal... right?" My voice sounded a little more high-pitched than I had intended. Way to keep a cool head, Prescilla.

I glanced at Cary and saw him shaking his head and staring wide-eyed at the approaching crowd.

Okay, so if the incubus was afraid of the horny toads approaching me, then maybe my concern was justified.

Meemo and Gray turned and pulled me with them.

Back into the fucking school.

Jack flipped the lock above the door, but we didn't stop moving. That wasn't the only entrance to this building, after all.

"Let's get to the professor's office. It has an industrial lock.

Maybe we can find some clues for whatever is going on here." Cary didn't wait for us to agree before he took off.

Memmo picked me up, and we all ran.

Yeah…

Definitely didn't think I would wake up today and deal with a horde of people wanting to fuck me.

How lucky could one girl get?

We'd better find answers because if not…

Well, I wasn't willing to fuck my way out of here, that's for sure.

Even my vagina shuddered in fear at the thought.

"It's okay, girl. I won't do that to you." I murmured.

Meemo, so comfortable running that he didn't even pant, interrupted my weird line of thinking. "Who are you talking to?"

Fuck! I must have said that out loud.

"Uh, no one. Just… thinking out loud?"

Meemo's brows pinched together, but he didn't say anything else.

We made it to the professor's office, and the door slammed shut behind us. The locks were put in place, and Jack pushed a large bookcase in front of it.

We heard sounds from behind the door. Instead of pounding, trying to break the door down to get to me, it sounded like… slapping?

And then moaning.

Oh my god, they were fucking in the halls!

We heard some of them peak and then… here was the kicker… they called out *my* name when they came.

"I have never been so equally flattered and completely disgusted in my entire life. Am I right?"

I turned to my guys, but they seemed to be dealing with their own struggles.

All of them were still sporting massively impressive stiffies, and they all looked just as hungry as the people on the campus green.

I gulped and hit reverse, smacking my back on the bookshelf.

"Prescilla, we have a small problem here," Cary finally said to me.

Oh no.

Nothing small at all about this problem.

I did not want to fuck my way off campus, but that didn't mean I would be against the idea of fucking my way around this room.

My vagina throbbed again.

"I'm sorry, girl. I may have spoken too soon."

I throbbed again, and this time I felt my wetness spreading.

I mean, I guess if I needed to take one for the team…

No better way to go out. Right?

Thanks for taking a chance on our second Chaos at PolyTech University *book! We'd love for you to leave us a review at your favorite e-book retailer.*

ACKNOWLEDGMENTS

As always, to our very long-suffering editor. We couldn't do this without you. We're sorry we were so chaotic that you got sick this time around.

Our husbands are our bedrocks. We couldn't do half of what we do without them. Thank you, guys!

To our Squad. Thank you for all of the tears (both heartache and joy). You all are our light.

ABOUT CASSANDRA JOY

Cassandra Joy is an author of adventure reverse harem romances. She's an avid reader of most every type of romance, but loves steamy MM action and one woman being pleasured by multiple men the most.

While Cassandra loves fantasizing about just such delicious stories, she's happily married to a single man. He's the father and manager of her brood of crazy offspring. They also have a fat cat that thinks he's a guard dog.

Sign up for Cassandra's newsletter to get notifications about upcoming books. You can find Cassandra at CassandraJoy.us or on any of these sites:

ABOUT G.R. LOREWEAVER

G.R. Loreweaver is an author of paranormal romance, twisted fairy tales, and so much more. She specializes in the witty-sexy side of menage and reverse harem.

G.R. loves sweary words, gaming, and debating why tacos are the perfection of food.

You can usually find G.R. and her shenanigans on Facebook in Loreweaver's Literary Lair. More information about G.R., her books, and her awesome team is available at GRLoreweaver.com

ALSO BY CASSANDRA JOY

CJ'S NEIGHBORHOOD SERIES

Dawn of a New Day

A Touch of Sunshine

Out of the Fire

Second Chance at Romance

QUICKIES IN CJ'S NEIGHBORHOOD

Dark Glimmer of Hope

Christmas Lights

Long Awaited

Summer Fun

The Fucked Up Fucking

Christmas on the Range

CHAOS AT POLYTECH UNIVERSITY

(with G.R. Loreweaver)

Death & Chaos

Longing & Chaos

Lust & Chaos

Trial & Chaos (March 2023)

Love & Chaos (April 2023)

AX TO THE HEART

Finding His Heart
Finding His Mage (June 2023)
Finding His Forever (September 2023)

ANTHOLOGIES

A Whale of a Time
Playing for Keeps (August 2023)

ALSO BY G.R. LOREWEAVER

NOCTIFER WITCH SERIES

Noctifer Magick
Noctifer Soul
Noctifer Heart
Noctifer Legacy (January 2023)

CHAOS AT POLYTECH UNIVERSITY

(with Cassandra Joy)
Death & Chaos
Longing & Chaos
Lust & Chaos
Trial & Chaos (March 2023)
Love & Chaos (April 2023)

A MYTH OF DIRE CONSEQUENCES

A Story of Lust & Deceit (May 2023)

ANTHOLOGIES

Once Upon an Ever After
A Whale of a Time
Lunar Rising
Celestial Awakening (June 2023)
Saved by the Every Day Hero (August 2023)

Made in the USA
Columbia, SC
22 January 2023